Natural Inclinations

Roland H. Wauer

Natural Inclinations

One
Man's
Adventures
in the
Natural
World

To order additional copies of this book, contact:
Xlibris
1-888-795-4274
www.Xlibris.com
Orders@Xlibris.com
765653

Introduction

Natural Inclination is an historic novel that is based on people I have known and places I have seen over the last many years. It also includes places that I have only wanted to visit but only learned about by reading pertinent materials. I became a mystical traveler that went places I could never afford or was never provided the opportunity.

Many of the chapters in *Natural Inclinations* are based upon friends and biologists that I have encountered along the way. As a biologist, a long-time birder, and lover of new and wild country, much of the experiences that Gregory Stewart had could only occur to such an adventurer.

Much of my story evolves around St. Croix in the Virgin Islands because I lived and worked there for several years and was able to visit all the Caribbean Islands as well as areas in Central America. I therefore utilized some of my wildlife encounters from that period of time.

The manuscript for *Natural Inclinations* has taken many years, starting more than a dozen years ago, after leaving St. Croix. I left the early chapter drafts untouched until a few months ago when I pulled it out of the drawer and read what I had first produced. I then realized that it could be a good story but needed to be tightened up and finished. That effort started slow but gradually increased in intensity. I present it here as a completed story although a good deal is a figment of my imagination.

Although my wife, Betty, had helped edit the initial chapters, she had passed away in 2013 and was not available to help with the later chapters. So, I gradually worked through it chapter by chapter, and I found help from my daughter-in-law, LeeAnn Nichols, especially with her knowledge of computers. I thank her for that vital assistance.

Chapter 1

Gathering all the courage that a naive 18-year-old can muster, I knocked on the door. Nothing. Yet, I knew that the great doctor was inside. I had seen him enter his office less than 20 minutes before, and I had not seen him exit. All the while I had been standing just down the hall, trying to find the courage to ask if I could participate in his expedition to Panama.

But what could a youth, barely out of high school and working as a part-time janitor in the Department of Preparation at the American Museum, offer? I had recently assisted in the preparation of study skins, and I had been learning to prepare animal mounts. But, after all, I was truly wet behind the ears. I had little more to offer. How could I expect to become a working member of Dr. Johnathan Lehman's Panama Expedition?

I knocked again. There was immediate response, "Yes?" It was obvious that he was perturbed at being bothered. I came very close to running away down the hall to the comfort of my closet and brooms. I took a deep breathe and entered.

Dr. Lehman's back was all I could see of the famous man, who sat behind a huge wooden desk, piled with books and papers. There was a faint mothball-like smell, and the walls were lined with books. A double set of specimen cabinets were situated in one corner of the office, one with an open door and a tray pulled out a foot or more. An old leather chair, piled with books, sat beside the desk. There was little room for anything more.

"Yes?" he asked again, even less civil than before. He unquestionably was aggravated at being disturbed. And he continued his examination of a bird specimen on a little table by his desk. I could barely see the bird, although from its bright green plumage, I guessed it to be a parrot.

It seemed like an eternity before I could speak. Finally, I heard myself saying, "Excuse me, Dr. Lehman, sir." I could feel my throat begin to tighten, but I continued: "My name is Gregory Stewart and I work with Dr. Jones downstairs in the Department of Preparation." I choked slightly, cleared my throat, and continued. "I understand that you are getting together an expedition to Panama. And if you have any room, I would like to join your expedition."

Without even turning around, Lehman curtly answered, "It's a small expedition and we're filled up." And he continued his study of the specimen before him. Out of nowhere, I said, "Dr. Lehman, do any of you speak Spanish?" Suddenly, he spun around in his chair and, looking directly at me, he said, "No, do you?" "Yes, sir, I do," I answered. He looked huge, staring over his desk at me. All I could think about was the many rumors of how difficult this man was to get along with, that he never liked to be corrected, and what he said was absolute law.

"Well," he said, slightly less curtly than before. "How old are you?" I gulped, and answered, "Nineteen, sir. Ah, I will be soon. I can prepare birds, and I am an excellent shot." He continued to study me over his glasses. Finally, he asked, "Where did you learn to speak Spanish?" I immediately responded, "In Puerto Rico, sir. I lived there for six years; I am from St. Croix in the Virgin Islands." He stared at me another minute or two, and then, as if to close the matter and to get back to work, he said: "I will think about it." He turned his back to me and began to examine the specimen before him.

Realizing that I was excused, or to put it more succinctly, he was finished with my interview; I was expected to leave. "Thank you, sir," I said. "I promise to work hard and I would not be a burden." I backed up to the open door and left, closing it behind me.

I stood outside in the hall, not knowing if my future as an ornithologist was over, or if it was just beginning. The remainder of the afternoon was only a blur; all I could think about was my meeting with Dr. Lehman and the chance that I might be joining the Panama Expedition.

I had been looking forward to Saturday afternoon all week; I was going to take Marjory to a movie theater. Marjory was visiting her aunt, Beatrice Johanson, who owned and operated the rooming house where I was living. Marjory and I had spent the previous Sunday together, talking about school, New York, and various other things that teenagers talk about when getting acquainted. And when I asked her to go to a movie the following Saturday, she had readily accepted, after receiving a quick approval from Aunt Bea. But now, with the possibility that I might go to Panama in a few weeks, my mind was centered primarily on that potential trip to Central America.

Friday evening at supper, I could not hide my excitement about my possible adventure, and I told Mrs. Johanson, Marjory, and the two other boarders about the day's events. Mrs. Johanson asked me several questions about the expedition, but once she understood that I had not yet been actually accepted, she dropped the matter. I am sure that she, and everyone else at the table, for that matter, thought that it was only a pipedream, that I would not be accepted.

I had moved into Mrs. Johanson's brownstone in early summer, soon after graduation. When I had first arrived in New York, I had moved downtown into a small hotel, after my mother returned to St. Croix. It was only after her strong objections and agreeing to return to St. Croix if I could not find work before the $25 she left me ran out. I had agreed to return on the *Guayana* when it was next in port, in about five weeks. The ship's purser was a close friend of my stepfather's. He had helped us with our initial trip to New York. He had even accompanied us to Mt. Hermann, where I was to board at my father's sister's home while attending high school. Mother had returned to St. Croix soon after I settled in and began schooling. She had come back to New York only once, to see me graduate.

My hotel room, on the third floor and overlooking a dark alley, was tiny, but clean. It contained only a bed, a dresser, a small table and chair, and, in one corner, was a huge pile of rope. However, what was most memorable about that room was the elevated train tracks situated less than a half-block away. Every 15 minutes a train would pass by, and the loud "clacck-t-clack-clack" noise was excruciating. But for one dollar a night, I didn't think that I could find anything better at the time. The longer I could hold out money-wise, the better chance I had of finding work.

That first morning, when I went down stairs, I asked the elderly gentleman at the little desk where I could get a cup of coffee. He looked me over and said, "Well, sir, you must be the lad that registered yesterday. Hopin' to find work are ye?"

"Yes, sir," I said. "I need to find something soon, before my money runs out. Do you have any suggestions?"

"Young man," he said, "I feel confident that ye will find something. Tis a big city, and thore's lots of work. What experience do ye have?"

I explained that I had just finished high school, and that the only work I had done in the past was helping with the growing and harvesting of sugar cane. With that, he looked at me and very seriously said, "Tis doubtful, ye know, that your experience with sugar cane will help ye very much in New York. But," he added, "If ye need a cheaper room, you might try Mrs. Johanson's Boarding House. Tis over on 76th, near the American Museum. Mrs. Johanson was originally from one of the islands, and she has helped others get started."

The idea of a cheaper room was not as interesting to me as its proximity to the American Museum. To me, the American Museum was one of the most exciting places in all of New York. I had visited its great animal halls on a couple earlier occasions, and I had every intention to do so again. The idea of living nearby, and even, perhaps, obtaining work there, was more than I could hope for. I decided to investigate Mrs. Johanson's Boarding House immediately.

"Sir," I said, "I am most interested in the boarding house. Would you kindly draw me a map to help me find my way?" Within a few minutes, I had a map in hand and was en route to Mrs. Johanson's, the American Museum, and any other site of interest in the vicinity, including a coffee shop just down the street. As I thanked the man at the desk, I remembered the pile of rope in my room. "By the way," I said, "that pile of rope that's in my room up there..." He started to laugh, and then he said, "Lad, the rope is to save ye from burnin' to death. If thare's a fire, ye tie it to the bed and throw the other end ut the window. Then ye climb ut the window and down the rope. Every room has one."

It was perfectly clear what was intended, but I wondered if I truly could have climbed down three stories on a rope.

The coffee shop was busy, but I found a seat at the counter and ordered coffee and a biscuit for five cents. The racial mix of customers was truly amazing. As I ate my breakfast I tried to guess where each had originated. I was reasonably sure there were Germans, Frenchmen, Norwegians, Spaniards, and a few Negroes. I wondered if any of these latter folks had come from the West Indies. It was truly a mix of cultures.

Then, using my new map, I started out in search for Mrs. Johanson's Boarding House. The walk was filled with new sights and sounds. New York in 1923 offered everything imaginable to a young man on his own for the very first time. But the American Museum was my lodestone. Over the years, I had not only read everything I could find about this great museum, but my stepfather had told me numerous stories about the great treasures it contained. With his tutelage in the Virgin Islands and Puerto Rico, I had become a pretty good naturalist, and I was anxious to see everything the natural history museum had to offer.

I never did reach the boarding house that first day. The enormous buildings of the American Museum got in the way. And by the time I had digested only a small part of the exhibits, it was closing time, time to walk back the 40 or more blocks to my hotel room that I already had paid for. As I left the building, I struck up a conversation with one of the guards, an Irish gentleman, who said that he had worked at the museum for "most of 18 years." I don't remember his name anymore, but when I asked him about possibly working at the museum, he told me that he had heard that Dr. Henery, the man in charge of exhibits, was looking for someone who could help with relabelling birds from an exhibit that had recently been replaced. I told the guard that relabelling birds was something that I could do, and that I would return the next day to talk with Dr. Henery.

En route back to my hotel, I ate at the same coffee shop. I was starving, as I hadn't eaten a thing since that morning's coffee and biscuit. The natural history exhibits had made me loose all sense of time.

The following morning, I again stopped for coffee and a biscuit, and then walked back to the American Museum. I arrived there just as the guards were opening the front doors, and I soon caught sight of my friend from the previous day. And within a very short time he had taken me into the back halls to the office of Dr. Henery.

Although Dr. Henery had already arrived at work, he was elsewhere; his secretary informed me that he would be back fairly soon. And she also confirmed the fact that, "Yes, Dr. Henery is looking for someone to help with the relabelling project."

I didn't have very long to wait before a middle-aged gentlemen arrived. I was introduced, and he invited me into his office. "I have been told that you might have work for me," I said, once inside. I added: "I have some training in ornithology, and I would be honored to assist you with relabelling birds."

Dr. Henery looked me over and asked me about my "experience." I admitted that all my ornithological training had been obtained from my stepfather, but he had taught me to make study skins of birds and mammals that we shot, and to label all the specimens with great care. I added that my Fredricksted teacher had used the specimens to teach the younger students about Virgin Island's wildlife.

He then asked me where I was living. I told him that my mother had left me in New York with only enough money to last for a few weeks, and that I hoped to find work before my money ran out. I explained that I had promised my mother that if I was not working soon that I would return to St. Croix on the *Guayana*, when it was next in port. He then asked me why I had finished my schooling in New York, and I explained that education in the Virgin Islands ceased by the time a boy was 15, 16 or 17, and one either sought a job or more education elsewhere. "My mother and stepfather wanted me to finish high school, and they made arrangements with my aunt, who lives in Mt. Herman, for me to stay with her and finish my schooling."

"Mr. Stewart," he said, as he handed me a blank specimen label and a pen, "please make out this label for one of your Virgin Island bird specimens." His request was obviously a test of my knowledge and ability. I chose a mountain dove, one of my favorite Virgin Islands' birds, and soon had written out a neat label. Handing it back to Dr. Henery, he looked it over very carefully, as if it was the real thing, and then said, "This job can be very tiresome, and we cannot tolerate mistakes." He paused, as if he was making a grave decision. Then he asked, "When would you be able to go to work?"

"Thank you, sir," I said. "I could go to work immediately, like right now." Dr. Henery chuckled and said, "Not today, Mr. Stewart, but if you will return tomorrow morning at 8:00 a.m., I will sign you up and you can begin."

I, of course, was elated. Not only had I found a job, but I was to work with birds at the American Museum. Nothing could have been better! And in my excitement, I forgot to ask about the salary that I would receive or the hours I would be expected to work, or anything else about the job. As far as I was concerned, I was employed at the American Museum. I probably would have worked for nothing. But as it was, I received the very munificent sum of one dollar a day.

I immediately found my guard friend to tell him my good fortune, and he seemed genuinely pleased that I had found work. As I left the building that day, I stood outside for a full half-hour, just looking over the great structure, with its ornate features and all. It seemed to me that all of the hard work in getting an education and learning about wildlife had been worthwhile. I was an employee of the American Museum of Natural History.

Mrs. Johanson's Boarding House was only about four blocks away, a perfect location for me. Mrs. Johanson turned out to be an elderly English widow who had moved to New York with her husband from St. Vincent, in the Leeward Islands. Her husband had died a few years later, leaving her with the brownstone and very little more. She was able to fix up four guest rooms that she rented only to men, and everyone ate together in her dining room. And as luck would have it, one of the rooms was vacant.

We immediately struck up a rapport, probably because I was a white West Indian. She agreed to rent me the room for $8 a month, and I also was expected to pay extra for each meal. Before the day was over I had moved all of my belongings, little more than a suitcase and a coat for cold weather, from the hotel to my new quarters.

Early the next morning I was waiting at the employee's entrance at the back of the American Museum. That first day, when I walked through that door, was, emotionally, one of the greatest days in my life. Life's dream had come to me practically out of nowhere. I never thought I would have such luck.

After completing some paper work and a short indoctrination, I was taken to the preparation room, where an entire wall was filled with boxes containing bird study skins. Those specimens had been part of an enormous display on birds from all parts of the world that had recently been updated with brighter, mounted birds. The old specimens had already been cleaned and placed in decontamination chambers to kill any possible domestus beetles that might have attacked the specimens while they were on display. My job was to copy every specimen tag, still on each bird, so that each specimen would possess both the faded original as well as the fresh copy. Then I was to place each in their proper tray in the specimen cabinets. It was a job that provided a wonderful opportunity, not only to study specimens from all parts of the world, but also to examine additional specimens that had not been displayed. It was a task that I was to finish in about three months time.

I suppose that almost anyone else relabeling about 2,000 bird skins would have become bored with such a task. But I remained fascinated throughout. I took great advantage of my job and learned all that I could about the specimens that I relabelled as well as other related specimens that I handled in the course of placing them is their proper locations.

About half-way through my relabeling job, I had the good fortune to meet Dr. Carl Jones, the great African explorer. It was during the time that I was relabelling the African species.

"Mr. Stewart, I would like to see the hornbills. Have you completed those birds as yet?" I had not noticed him come into the room, and I did not realize that he was present until he spoke, only a foot or two away. I was startled by his booming voice. And when I turned and discovered who it was, I was doubly startled. Although someone had previously pointed him out to me, I had never before been so close to the great man.

"Yes, sir," I stammered, "I completed all the hornbills and put them away." Then, I added, "But I believe that the black-casqued hornbill is incorrectly labeled; it was labeled as a female, but I think it is an immature male." He suddenly looked more carefully at me. I was unsure whether to excuse myself and beat a hasty retreat, or to apologize for being so insensitive. But without any hesitancy, he said, "Congratulations, young man, you are correct. I noticed the error myself. I was not able to make the correction in the exhibit, but the label must be corrected before it is put away. Let's make the change immediately."

With that, he walked to the cabinet containing hornbills. I open the door, and pulled out the proper tray. Dr. Jones picked up the correct specimen and announced, "We must not change the original tag, but if you will redo the new tag, I will initial the change in sex." Within a very few minutes I had written the new tag as requested, Dr. Jones initialed it, and replaced the specimen in the draw. He then turned to me again. "Mr. Stewart, I can see that you do very neat work, and you apparently also have a good eye for birds. Where did you learn your skills?"

"Sir," I answered, I don't have any formal training, but I learned about wildlife and how to make study skins from my stepfather. We spent every Sunday together outdoors, hunting, fishing, and studying nature. He taught me everything I know."

Dr. Jones then asked, "Tell me, how did you know the hornbill sex was in error?" "The comparative bill size and the base of the bill was that of a young bird," I answered.

"You are very perceptive for so young a man," he said. I quickly explained that I had been taught to see whatever I was looking at. "At home, we would stand in the yard at night, and he, my stepfather, would ask how many stars I was seeing in a particular constellation. Like the Pleiades, the seven sisters. He would keep after me until I could see all seven stars. He explained that was how the American Indians trained their boys to see."

"You apparently had a very good teacher," Jones said. "And you also can prepare tags that are neat and legible. What do you plan to do when your current project is completed?" I realized then that I was half-way through my relabelling assignment, and I did not have another job after it was over. I answered, "I have no plans, sir, but I hoped that I could remain at the museum in another capacity."

Jones said, "When you finish up here, come and see me. I need a general cleanup man and someone who can help me with preparations." And with that he turned and walked out of the room.

And that's how I went to work for Dr. Carl Jones in the Department of Preparation. He had developed a completely new method of modeling birds and mammals. He first took very careful measurements of the animals. Then he made a clay model identical to the specimen and cast a paper mache model that was strong and light weight; the clay could later be reused. He then fitted the prepared skin over the paper mache model and sewed it up. Eventually he added glass eyes.

My new work for Dr. Jones provided me opportunities that I did not have while doing the relabelling. Besides learning the new technique of preparing bird and mammal mounts, I had a free run of the collections. I also was expected to sweep the floor and keep the rooms tidy and clean, but I didn't mind the janitorial work at all. It let me see every bit of the preparatory quarters. And, since I had few other obligations, I worked long hours, even helping Dr. Jones with various projects late into the night. It was a wonderful opportunity for a young West Indian.

Marjory was my only diversion during that period of my life. Although I had had a childhood sweetheart back on St. Croix, neither of us were mature enough to advance our relationship beyond holding hands and, after several weeks, an occasional kiss. And during my three years at Mt. Herman, none of the girls paid me much attention. But Marjory was a very different matter.

On Saturday afternoon, we walked to the movie theater, and sat in the balcony. Marjory said she preferred to watch a movie from that higher angle, and I could care less. My mind was still on my chance of going to Panama. However, Marjory had other things in mind. And the movie, itself, had little to do with the diversion.

Once we settled into our seats, even before the lights went out, Marjory took my hand and held it very tight. And as soon as the movie began, she ask me to put my arm around her, which I did immediately. We must have sat that way until intermission, holding my hand with both of hers and my free arm around her shoulders. She also had a way of snuggling extremely close and even laying her head on my shoulder.

Soon after intermission and the movie restarted, she asked me if I wanted to kiss her. I said I did, and we immediately touched lips in a short kiss. That first kiss seemed to break any reserve we might have had, because we spent all of the second half of the movie kissing. Now, from all my previous experience with kissing, it was something that two people sort of led up to with holding hands and some casual pecks. But that afternoon in the theater balcony, it seemed to me that we shared one long kiss. I must admit that I thoroughly enjoyed that closeness, and I even forgot for a brief time my dream of going to Panama. And if we had not promised her aunt that we would be back at a certain time, right after the movie, we might have stayed through a second showing. As it was, we left soon after the movie and walked back to Mrs. Johanson's hand-in-hand. I was in love for the first time.

On Sunday, I even accompanied Mrs. Johanson and Marjory to church. It was the first time that I had attended church in New York, although I had gone with my mother and stepfather occasionally in St. Croix. I was not much of a church-goer, and my attendance on that particular Sunday was only to be with Marjory. That Sunday was particularly enjoyable.

My weekend experiences remained on my mind throughout Monday morning. My cleanup work was done almost by rote, and I had a difficult time keeping my mind on my work. I even had begun to doubt the logic of being part of the Panama Expedition.

It was almost noon before I was told that Dr. Lehman wanted to see me. That second visit to the great man's office was not as scary as it had been three days earlier. He apparently was anticipating my arrival, and he immediately told me that I could go on the condition that I would not only serve as a translator, but also as a helper for everything else that might be required in camp. I agreed with whatever he said, and left that office with great anticipation for the journey that was to begin in only three weeks.

My relation with Marjory had been replaced with my zeal for Panama.

Chapter 2

Panama was all I had dreamed it would be. Our destination was the Chirique region, particularly the Volcan Chiriqui highlands and the upper drainage of the Rio Chiriqui. However, getting to this isolated area, on the Pacific slope in the far western corner of the country, was another matter.

Arriving by steamer at Panama's Atlantic port of Colon late one afternoon, we anchored inside the breakers that sheltered the waters of Colon from the Atlantic rollers. Although we all wanted to go ashore, we had to remain aboard until we had passed through the Canal and arrived in Panama City on the Pacific side. There was a lot of talk that evening about what each person would do once on shore. The sailors claimed that Panama City was a free port where one could acquire whatever was desired. Dr. Lehman and the other scientists talked only about the natural treasures they expected to find in the lush tropical forests that awaited us.

Mid-morning the following day a Canal pilot and eight natives came aboard; they were to help us navigate through the Canal. And within a very short time we were on our way. It was the first passage through the Panama Canal for all five members of our science party. The Canal had been opened less than ten years earlier, and it truly was something to marvel about. A magnificent shrine to man's technological achievement. Our captain who had been through the canal several times in the past, pointed out that "the French had begun the Canal in 1881, but it took United States engineers to complete the task. It was finally opened to traffic on August 15, 1914."

He further explained that "The Canal Zone, under the direction of the United States, is a strip of land five miles on either side of the Canal. And the U.S. maintains the Canal and lands within the Canal Zone." He added that "The U.S. also supervises the administration of both Colon and Panama City, as well as providing the Republic of Panama with protection against potential attacks." I found the Canal Zone well maintained and operated.

Once past the mighty Gutan Locks, we entered Lake Gatun that is said to be 85 feet above sea-level and the largest artificial lake in the world. Patches of jungle and dead trees protruded here and there from the lake surface. And as we passed Barro Colorado Island, a former hilltop, I overheard Dr. Lehman tell his colleagues that the entire island had only that year become a research station under the supervision of the Smithsonian Institution.

Passing through the locks was a unique experience. The ship's engines were stopped, and strong steel lines, pulled by electric locomotives called "mules," were used to slowly tow the ship. There was no shouting of instruction of any kind; it all was done by hand-given signals. Exceedingly smooth and efficient.

We reached Balboa, the port for Panama City, late that afternoon, and were soon walking about on stable ground once again. After 10 days aboard ship, it was most welcome. And before long we were comfortably settled at a nearby hotel. Although I can no longer remember the name of the hotel, supper that evening reminded me so much of the meals my mother served for guests at home in the Virgin Islands, and I had one of the few attacks of homesickness I can remember. Panama City reminded me so much of a gigantic Fredricksted, the West End town where I gone to school on St. Croix. But unlike Fredricksted, it was a busy, thriving city.

My thoughts of my homeland were soon forgotten as the discussion focused on the necessary preparations for our journey to David, more than 20 miles to the west, at the southern base of Volcan Chiriqui. The next day our small company of scientists began to purchase enough supplies that were to last throughout our six-week expedition to the Chirique highlands. My ability to speak Spanish helped a great deal during those negotiations, and I got my first taste of Panama City. By the end of our second day, we had such a huge pile of goods that I was unsure if we could ever get it all packed for transportation to David.

That evening I was introduced to Robert Beaman, who, unbeknown at the time, was to become my constant companion for the next several months. Beaman, I later learned, was an ex-navy man living in the city, who knew the country and the native people extremely well. He and Dr. Lehman had somehow got acquainted, and Lehman apparently had hired him to assist us with transportation and other activities. And as it turned out, Beaman also had a natural ability to locate some of the rarer bird species as well as making study skins. He was a wonderful addition to our party, and it was he who made arrangements for transporting the great pile of goods purchased in Panama City, as well as the collecting supplies that we brought with us, to David.

David, in 1923, was little more than an Indian village with a large Catholic church and about a dozen businesses operated by Spaniards. Although the acquisition of four pack mules was undertaken with little difficulty, Beaman insisted that we also hire an Indian guide. At first, Dr. Lehman did not agree on the value of such an individual, but Benson soon convinced him that it could be dangerous otherwise. "Dr. Lehman," he argued, "the Guaymis Indians, who live and control the Chirique high-country, do not trust white men. They believe that outsiders come only to find gold." Beaman further explained that the first Spaniards, who were initially welcomed by the Guaymis peoples, took advantage of their good will. They came only to find gold, and eventually slaughtered hundreds of Indians. "I am told that one of the Indian chiefs, a man known as Agusto, might be persuaded to guide our party," Beaman added.

It was soon agreed that Benson was to find Agusto, who was visiting relatives in a nearby village. And by the following evening the arrangements had been consummated. Beaman arrived back at our little camp, at the outskirts of David, late in the afternoon, and he immediately told us the good news. "Agusto has agreed to guide our party. But he had to be persuaded. He has only recently married, and he was visiting his wife's family. Agusto said he would not leave his new bride behind. So I told him that he could also take his wife, and that we would supply him with his own tent."

There was an immediate response from Dr. Lehman. "Mr. Beaman, you should not have obligated one of our tents; we only brought five, and they already have been allocated. One is for specimen preparation and storage, one for cooking, and the other three are required for sleeping. You must tell Agusto that we will not need his assistance." That response was followed by an uncomfortable silence.

It was Lehman's assistant, Mr. Gordon, our unofficial second-in-command that broke the silence. "Based on my conversations with some of the local people today, there is concern for our safety while in the mountains. A guide is not only essential, but to change our agreement now might be dangerous."

"What are our options?" Lehman demanded.

It was Beaman who supplied the answer. "It would be more practical to prepare specimens in a lean-to, where we would have greater air movement when working. We can make room in one of the sleeping tents for storage."

"Yes," Gordon added, "a logical solution."

Everyone seemed to agree, with the possible exception of Dr. Lehman. But little else was said. And in the end, the decision to take a guide may have saved our lives.

Two days later, with all of our materials and supplies packed on the four mules or in individual packs, which each of us carried, we left David on foot. Agusto and his wife took the lead, with Beaman and Dr. Lehman close behind. The four mules, led by two of Agusto's relatives drew up the rear. It seemed to me that the entire town of David came out to see us off.

We reached our base camp, situated at about 7,000 feet elevation on Volcan Chiriqui, late on the second day. Our route had passed through some magnificent forest and along clear, swift streams. We saw birds that I had never before seen in the wild. I was sure that many of them had never before been scientifically recorded. It was a marvelous beginning to our Chiriqui adventure. That day was the first time that I felt I was actually a member of Dr. Lehman's expedition, for we shared the excitement of the many new sights and sounds.

The site of our base camp was in a little valley at the foot of a long canyon filled with an amazing variety of vegetation. It reminded me of a huge greenhouse. As we pitched camp, bird sounds were all around us. And that evening, as we ate our first campsite meal, a resplendent quetzal displayed above the dense jungle growth nearby, howler monkey calls resounded from the forest in all direction, and after dark, ringtails and owls called from the nearby forest.

For two weeks we collected specimens during all the daylight hours, and spent long hours each evening preparing skins. It was hard work, but never had I enjoyed life so much as those days in the Chirique highlands. Even my camp chores, which kept me up even after everyone else had gone to bed, was enjoyable. The night sounds of mammals, birds and insects were a whole new world to me. It allowed my imagination to run wild trying to identify the perpetrators. Ever since those first nights in the Panamanian jungle, I have enjoyed night sounds whenever an opportunity arises.

Our Chirique expedition was only about one-third complete when suddenly, while preparing supper at dusk, a horseman came full-gallop into our compound. It was an Indian that Agusto immediately recognized as his brother, who was greatly excited and calling to his brother, even before he dismounted. It took only a short time before Agusto told us that his brother had come to warn us that our lives were in danger and that we must leave immediately. Agusto explained that many of the younger Guaymis Indians believed that our real reason for the interest in the area was to find gold; they thought our binoculars were magical tools that could look into the ground and find the precious metal. He also said that a large group of young men already were en route to our camp, and that if we were to survive, we would need to leave immediately.

Agusto was obviously distressed. He undoubtedly felt that he was responsible for our safety. Beaman quickly explained that the men heading our way were not part of Agusto's tribe, and that he had no control over their actions. It was abundantly clear that we must leave before they arrive.

Like madmen, we began to fold our camp. Dr. Lehman and Beaman took care of the hundred or more specimens we had so far collected, while the rest of us packed all our essential supplies onto three of the mules. The fourth mule was loaded with the specimen and preparation materials. In an amazingly short time we were loaded and ready to flee, although various items were left strewn about our campsite.

Off we went, in the dark of the night, following a different, narrow and slippery trail so that we would not encounter the party of young bucks that were headed our way. How we managed to get off that mountain, following that God-awful mountain trail, is anyone's guess. We had one serious incident. One of the pack mules bumped a second one that lost its footing and went screaming down a steep slope. The mule's high-pitched scream, as it fell several hundred feet to the bottom, where its screams suddenly ceased following a loud crash, remained with me for years afterward. But we didn't even stop to access the animal's fate or to retrieve the lost supplies.

We continued on at the same breakneck speed, following Agusto, his wife riding the one horse, and his brother. We had lost a lot of baggage when we lost our mule, but all our specimens were safe on another mule. And we reached David and safety the next day.

I have often wondered what would have happened to us if we had not hired Agusto as our guide. He and his brother had undoubtedly saved our lives, and we were most thankful, in spite of the premature closure of the expedition.

Dr. Lehman was highly upset, but rather than to risk our lives, he decided that we should all return to Panama City and then on to New York. It was a cheerless trip to Panama City, but even so, I suppose that our highly successful early collection from the Chiriqui highlands had made it all worthwhile.

In Panama City, we learned that a steamer would be passing through the Canal en route to New York in three days, and so arrangements were made for our return. However, I had been thinking about the possibility of remaining in Panama and continuing with specimen collections. I had talked with Beaman about this possibility, and he had agreed.

So, after dinner on the evening before we were to depart for New York, I asked, "Dr. Lehman, would you like me to remain here and finish collecting?"

Lehman looked at me again as if I was crazy, and said, "Stewart, I can't leave you here. It is too great a responsibility to leave you in Panama."

"Well, Sir," I said, "Beaman will be with me. Beaman and I will collect together. The supplies are already available, and we could arrange to collect at numerous other sites."

Dr. Lehman turned to Beaman, who was sitting across the table, said, "What are your plans? Could you continue with the collections?" Beaman immediately said that he could. I imagine that he was wondering where he was going to find work now that the Chiriqui Expedition had come to a halt. Lehman turned back to me and said, "That would be wonderful for you and Beaman to stay and finish up the collection." And that's what we did.

For almost a year after Dr. Lehman and the other ornithologists left for New York, Beaman and I collected birds throughout the Panamanian lowlands and even into a few upland sites, such as the Chagres River drainage. But we never returned to the Chiriqui country.

I had a wonderful time. Beaman and I got along very well, and he also got along well with the native people. He had a knack of getting their help in finding certain rare or shy birds. I learned then that the native people knew their environment much better than Beaman and I, or any other outsider could hope to. Although most of the folks we met in the field possessed little if any formal education, they more than compensated with their understanding of their surroundings. The Panamanians were some of the most resourceful and cheerful people I have ever met.

We began to travel around the countryside with a lone mule that carried all our camping gear and supplies. Finding a particular good bird area, we would remain for a few to several days until we had collected one or two specimens of all the new species present there. We also made rather extensive notes on all of the birds observed at each site, and that effort began to take more and more time as our knowledge of the bird life increased. Our problem, however, was our inability to identify many of the species. But we soon learned that the local people had their own name for each bird, and we begun to refer to the various species by using those names.

We spent the majority of the time in forested areas within the Canal Zone. Lands outside the zone were being cut for agriculture and grazing; banana plantations seemed to be of high priority and were started throughout. Greater opportunities for transporting bananas and other goods to other countries by way of the numerous ships that passed through the canal was plenty incentive for the enterprising Panamanians.

Our mornings were usually spent in collecting, and our afternoons were usually spent in the shade of make-shift thatched huts preparing specimens. Every two weeks we shipped the specimens to New York aboard one of the steamers. And we were then able to visit the bank to retrieve funds that had been sent there by the American Museum for our use.

We attracted considerable attention in the field, and it seemed that we always had a group if youngsters standing around, watching as we prepared the specimens. And occasionally, one of the boys would also go with us when collecting. Sometimes, these youngsters had considerable knowledge about a particular bird species.

We ate surprisingly well in the field. Parrots were commonplace, and we were especially interested in obtaining a representative collection. So, they often formed the basis of our meals. And we also had a continuous supply of tortillas, beans and rice. The local folks would gladly sell us fresh food whenever possible.

I am not really sure how I became involved with Suzana, but her younger brother had gone with us on a couple morning hunts. She appeared one evening with a plate of burritos, that she said was in payment for our kindness toward her brother. They were delicious. Suzana was an extraordinarily striking woman of about 16 or 17, with black eyes, a slender waist, lovely breasts, and an infectious smile. All during the remainder of our stay in that area, longer than initially intended, she brought us a daily token for taking an interest in her brother.

It had been several months since the last time I have even talked to a female my age, so I am sure that part of my need was just companionship with the opposite sex. We began spending each evening together, and she even seemed genuinely interested in the specimens that I prepared. And after I finished the preparations we talked late into the night. She told me that her mother had died a year earlier, and that she was taking care of her brother. Her father worked as a mechanic for some of the Americans who ran the Canal.

I fell madly in love with Suzana. And I believe that she, too, fell madly in love with me.

It was my first true love, and I had a terrible time leaving her for our next collecting site a few days later. But I returned to see her every two weeks en route back to Panama City to ship out specimens.

On one of those nights that I stayed over while Beaman continued on to the city, after Suzana's father left early that next morning for work, I could not resist any longer and brought Suzana to my bed. She was as eager as I, and our love was consummated in the early morning, with a soft rain falling on the thatched roof and the dawn chorus of birdsongs all around us.

Our relationship continued for so long as I was able to stop by for a visit. But Beaman and I eventually moved to an area west of Panama City, and so our lovemaking became less numerous and eventually she told me that she had another love. I found out a little later that she had married in the church. I was terribly shaken at the news, and I wanted to confront her in person, to ask her if she still loved me. Beaman strongly advised me against such action, and since we were working a day's hike away from her village, it never occurred.

Not long afterward, I began to feel poorly. I had a difficult time keeping my food down, and I developed a rash with tiny warts along my waistband. After several days without any letup, I went to a doctor in Panama City. He had not seen anything like my symptoms, but was sure that it was not any kind of venereal disease. The only thing I could think of at the time was the possibility that I had contracted something from Suzana. Yet, she had told me that I had been her first lover. Although I was reasonably confident that she had not lied to me, after hearing about her marriage I had some doubts.

It was only after a discussion with the doctor about my collecting activities that he diagnosed my problem as arsenic poisoning. I had been using arsenic as a preservative in the bird specimens. Some of the powder apparently had gathered at my waistband, since most of the preparation was done while wearing only shorts. Arsenic and a sweaty waistband had led to arsenic poisoning, a condition that would only worsen if I continued. I was told that I would have to refrain from any further work of that type for a few weeks. So, with regret, I decided to take a two-week rest to recover. I rented a cheap hotel room and decided that I would stay out of the field and see more of Panama City.

Beaman came by to check on me a few days later, when he shipped specimens, and we had supper together before he headed back to his camp. We had cabled Dr. Lehman about my illness and had received an immediate response stating that I was to return to New York as soon as possible. That was the last time I was to see Beaman.

Panama City was an amazing place. And I got to know the city extremely well. I apparently fit in very well, as I looked and dressed like the natives. I was fascinated with the Chiriqui Prison that had once been a Spanish fort, complete with dungeons, situated under the seawall promenade. And the Metropolitan Cathedral was an amazing piece of architecture. It had taken more that than 100 years to complete. The cathedral's towers are layered with mother-of-pearls and shined brightly in the sunlight.

But I spent much of my time those few days in Panama City at the docks, principally because of the marvelous three-masted barquentine, the *St. Maria*, that was docked there. I had never seen such as exquisite ship.

I soon became acquainted with several of the ship's sailors, and learned that the *St. Maria* was a British ship under contract with the National Scientific Research Association. She was headed for the South Seas for a scientific expedition and would be gone for about one year. The expedition included scientists in every field, from mammalogy to entomology, botany and geology. The ornithologist was a Major J. J. Johnson. I knew right away that somehow I would be going to the South Seas.

I returned to the dock that evening when the men were going ashore. Several of the sailors were about my age, and since I knew the city I naturally took them all around. One of the men, Henny something or other, became very chummy. It was he who told me about all their destinations; first the Galapagos, later the Marquesas and the Societys. It would be a dream come true.

"Henny," I said, "how about I join the expedition?" "I don't know," he answered. "I'm told we've a full complement. Ye could talk to the captain, Mr. Bonney."

The very next day I went aboard with Henny and introduced myself to Captain Bonney. I said, "Captain Bonney, as you can see I'm a young man. But all my life I've dreamt of going to the Pacific. It's the dream of my life. If you take me, I will cause no trouble, and I'll work hard. I don't want a penny; just give me a little food." I explained what I been doing in Panama, and that I could be a big help to him in a number of ways. Captain Bonney told me that he was sorry but they had no room. And in spite of my pleas and offer to help in every way possible, the answer remained the same.

So I continued to hang around with Henny and some of the other men, and each day I was on the ship, even working alongside the others. If there was anything to do I did it. Finally, realizing that the captain was not going to change his mind, I told Henny that I had a plan.

"What plan do ye have?" he asked. "Well," I said, "I will sneak aboard the night you all sail and hide in one of the empty life boats under the canvas. I'll stay there until we are several hundred miles out to sea. Captain Bonney is not going to throw me overboard, and he won't turn back. He's going to cuss and raise hell, but that's all he's going to do. But," I added, "You will need to provide me a little food and water each evening. Will you help?"

Henny looked at me for a long time, then he got this strange grin on his face and said, "Sounds like fun, mate. Sure ye can depend on me, once aboard." And with that, I had decided what to do. I was going to go to the South Seas, that's all there was to it.

But the next day, while the crew was preparing for sailing that night, I went back to the captain to beg him one more time. "Captain Bonney, please take me," I pleaded. "On a sailing ship, there always is need for another experienced hand."

Then, out of the blue, he said, "OK, Stewart, but on one condition." My mouth must have dropped, because he grinned at me in a strange manner. Then he said, "You must accompany Ms. Clouster, our entomologist, wherever she goes. You must see to it that she does not get lost or take off by herself. And she must believe that you want to learn about bugs. She must not suspect anything, or she would never consent." I immediately agreed to whatever demands the captain might add.

Later I learned that the captain had earlier told Ms. Clouster that he had met a young man who was very interested in insects and begging to go along, who could help her with her collecting activities. If she agreed, he would add another person to the ship's roster. I apparently had been a Godsend to the captain, who had little use for Ms. Clouster. She was a very peculiar sort of individual. She had no use for men. She lived her life entirely alone with her insects. But she, apparently, was a very well-known British entomologist.

Within the hour I found a bunk in the foscel near that of my friend Henny's. And the remained of the day was spent retrieving what little clothes and other materials I had at the hotel, and leaving a note for Beaman.

"Beaman, "I wrote, "I have the extreme good fortune to sail for the South Seas on the *St. Maria*, with the British Museum Expedition. We will be collecting specimens throughout the Southern Pacific. I leave tonight, April 26, and will be gone for about one year. Please inform Dr. Lehman about my decision. I have enjoyed our companionship, and I hope that you continue to be well. Your friend, Gregory Stewart."

Chapter 3

The *St. Maria* set off from Balboa on June 26, and reached the Pearl Islands the very next day. We anchored in the quiet waters of St. Elmos's Bay at Isla de Rey, the largest of the Pearls. These islands once were famed for the abundant pearl oysters that lived there. But the early Spaniards, in their greed for riches, practically destroyed that entire resource. The current oyster fishery no longer was able to support the native peoples, much less the settlers from the mainland who had taken control of both the fishery and what little agriculture lands the island possessed. I found the Pearl Islands to be an extremely impoverished environment.

The Isla de Rey villages were little more than ragged huts and the peoples poorly maintained. In fact, throughout our two-day stay, our ship's medical doctor, Dr. Jensen, spent all of his time caring for the sick. Those people had no medical supplies at all, so our presence was most welcome.

During our stay at Isla de Rey the scientists were able to collect a variety of specimens, although we were too near the mainland for any startling discoveries. Ms. Clouster apparently decided that it was time to begin my indoctrination about my expected duties in the coming weeks.

"Stewart," she said, "you shall accompany me whenever and wherever I go afield." All during the trip she addressed me by my last name and always seemed to put me in my place as her lackey that would be at her beckon-call. Although I resented her attitude, I was grateful for the opportunity to participate in the expedition.

That first morning, after being rowed ashore by two of the sailors, we set off into the adjacent jungle. She carried a butterfly net and a light shoulder pack, while I carried an extremely heavy pack stuffed with specimen jars filled with alcohol as well as the day's lunches.

Our collecting started out rather well that first day. We made an extended loop across the island and returned two miles or more down the beach from the village, where we found our intended route blocked by a magnificent stand of mangroves.

We could hear the waves lapping the shore on the far side of the mangroves, and Ms. Clouster decided that we should cut through the mangroves. She decided that we could cut through the stand and follow the beach back to the village. But having grown up in the vicinity of mangroves in the Virgin Islands, I knew that those mangroves could be a mile across and include several sizable streams. I thought our easiest route might be to retrace part of our route and stay out of the mangroves. The tide was rising, and a mangrove swamp is not a good place to be at any time, much less when it begins to fill with water.

"Ms. Clouster," I said, "I believe that we had best retrace part of our route, rather than to try to find a way through these mangroves." Although she had been curt but helpful throughout the day, even identifying various insect families that we had collected, her attitude changed immediately.

Apparently thinking that I was questioning her superiority, she tartly responded, "Mr. Stewart, this swamp is a small one; we can cross it in no time." And without another word, she was off, wading into the black mud. I, of course, followed behind her with my load of jars.

The going was extremely slow, as we were forced to pull each foot out of the muck, with a loud sucking noise at every step. Suddenly we found the way barred by a wide stream. But since our goal seemed to be just the other side, she boldly began to wade across. It was soon obvious to me that the stream was deeper than she expected, because the water was up to my waist before we were a quarter of the way across, and I was a good foot taller than she. And before she was half-way across, Ms. Clouster found herself in real difficulty and began to flounder, not able to stay upright. I immediately went to her rescue, and physically had to pull her back to shallower water where she could again find adequate footing.

"It is too deep at this crossing," she then announced, without any sort of thank you. "We will walk up a short distance and try once more there." With that, she was off again, with me and my pack, which had become soaked, making it even heavier, in pursuit. In a couple hundred yards, she decided to try again, and once more began to cross the stream. This time she had gone only about 30 feet before she sunk down into a hole so that only her shoulders and head were above water. Her butterfly net floated away down-stream.

If I had not reached out and held her up, she would have gone completely underwater. As it was, one strap of my pack broke and several jars were lost.

It took we several minutes to gradually help her back to where she had started across, and several more minutes before she could repair the pack to where it would not loose any additional specimens. All the while she was telling me that I was at fault for the broken pack strap and loss of the jars, and that I would need to be more careful. However, she then agreed to retrace our route to where we would not need to negotiate the mangrove swamp.

It took us a good part of two hours, traveling at a snail's pace, to where we finally sighted the village and our waiting boat. We arrived back on the *St. Maria* just before dark, covered with gooey, black muck and extremely tired from our day's adventures. And not once did Ms. Clouster admit to her errors. It was abundantly obvious why I had been allowed to join the expedition.

Mid-morning of June 28, we left the Pearl Islands, sailing southward, and arrived at the little island of Gorgona five days later. On the second day out, Captain Bonney approached me on deck, "Mr. Stewart, you and Ms. Clouster looked rather dirty and tired after your collecting trip on Isla de Rey. Did you enjoy your day?" he asked with a grin.

"Sir," I answered, "we had a terrible time trying to get through the mangrove swamp."

Still grinning, he said, "And I suppose, after growing up with mangroves, that it was your idea?" "No, sir," I said. He grinned and walked away,

Gorgona, located just off the South American coast from Columbia, was not on the original list of places to visit, according to Mr. Graff, the expedition's mammalogist. In fact, as Mr. Graff pointed out, "Except for introduced European rats, pigs and goats, mammals are few and far between on the islands of the South Seas." However, Mr. Graff had heard rumors of a new monkey, a new agouti, and a native rat that were suppose to reside on Gorgona, undoubtedly due to its close proximity to the continent. And he intended to collect specimens of each.

We remained at Gorgona a full week, and it, unexpectedly, was one of our most pleasant stops on the entire voyage. We anchored in a quiet stretch of water about a half-mile off the Columbian coast, between the island and the mainland. The high Andes formed an immense backdrop to the west. On clear days, the snowy peaks and the green-clad jungle in the foreground provided us with an incredibly beautiful scene. And at night the air was filled with the sounds of millions of frogs, their plaintive cries resounded across the water. Their haunting cries seemed to arouse one's sympathy.

The haunting frog songs, however, created odd behavior with the sailors. Henny explained that one of the older sailors, originally from Haiti, believed that frog songs were long-dead sailors that had been vanquished to the isolated coastline centuries earlier. "Greg," he said, "the old Haitian said that the sounds were of dead sailors, wanting passage home."

A few of the other sailors agreed with him. I wasn't sure where Henny stood. But he was not relieved until I collected one of the frogs. I brought it back to the ship, placed it in a tub of tepid water, and it soon began to sing. Even then, the Haitian sailor was sure that the frog was one of the long-dead souls, and it was on-board. By the next morning the frog had disappeared. Whether it had crawled out of the tub and jumped off the ship, or if a Haitian sailor had thrown it overboard remained a mystery.

Early the first full day on Gorgona, all of the scientists went ashore in search of their special interests. Just beyond the beach was a forest filled with enormous ferns and gigantic horsetails and club-mosses. It was the most exquisite tropical forest that I ever encountered. And all during our stay, we saw no other humans, although we discovered the remains of a long-deserted plantation, including a deserted bungalow.

That first evening we all came back with one success story after the other, except for Mr. Graff, as he had failed to find any of his target species. However, Ms. Clouster and I had encountered a small troop of moneys along a little river at midday. I had admired them as they chattered high over our heads. And one of those monkeys had even pelted us with nuts. Without a gun, I was unable to collect one. My collecting equipment included only a butterfly net and the tweezers for certain biting insects.

When we reported the monkeys to Mr. Graff, he got very excited, and he asked Ms. Clouster if he could borrow me the next day to help him find the monkeys. Since we had collected a huge number of insects that first day, and she already planned to stay aboard and prepare her specimens the next day, she readily agreed. And so the following day was scheduled for a visit to "Monkey River," the name that we all began to use for the river where we had encountered the monkeys.

Ms. Clouster retired very early every evening, soon after super, and since I had no further assignments, I asked Major Johnson that evening if he would like me to help him prepare bird skins. He had collected about four dozen specimens during the day on Gorgona, and he and his assistant were extremely busy with the specimens. "Mr. Stewart, have you prepared skins before," he asked. And when I told him about my experience at the

American Museum and in Panama, he readily accepted my help. He was even more pleased when he saw the final product and the speed in which I worked. In fact, if I say so myself, my specimens were much better than his companion, although, until now, I never did tell anyone. So preparing bird skins became my regular activity thereafter. And later, I even overheard Johnson compliment my preparation skills to Captain Bonney.

All of the skins were prepared on-deck, where there was a constant breeze. It was a far cry from the hot, muggy sites I had experienced in the Panamanian jungle. And instead of using arsenic, the skins were lightly salted for protection against domestus beetles.

On one of those first evenings, while preparing skins, Henny expressed interest in helping. "Ye need help?" he asked. Mr. Johnson looked up from a woodpecker skin he was preparing. "Have you prepared skins before?"

"No, sir," Henny responded. "But I could learn."

"We don't have extra specimens to teach you," Johnson said, in a rather curt manner.

"Sir," I said, "I would be glad to help Henny. He could watch me, and I would watch over his first skins."

"Mr. Stewart," Johnson responded, "everyone on the ship has his own responsibilities. Captain Bonney would not agree to one of his sailors helping us with our duties."

I decided that it was best to drop the issue for now. But I later told Henny that if he really was interested that I would find a way to get him involved. "No," he said, "I know me place; I won't ask ye to help." After that, Henny never again approached our preparation area.

The morning of May 5 found our small party of explorers back on the beach and en route to Monkey River. Once we arrived at the river, that was a fast flowing stream with slippery bounders, we decided that we would have better luck with finding monkeys by slowly wading the stream rather than noisily hacking our way along the jungle-dominated stream bank. But on several occasions we encountered a rockfall that required a detour up and around via steep banks. It was not an easy task.

After one such detour, while sitting on rocks at the edge of the stream, trying to regain our energy, I detected a very brief movement in the high foliage a short distance up-stream. "Major," I said, "I think there are monkeys directly ahead of us over the stream."

We all froze in place, searching the high branches. Then, a monkey moved high overhead even closer and behind us, and a second later Major

Johnson fired both barrels of his gun in rapid succession. Two hairy black-and-white bodies came tumbling down from the trees. One landed not more than 150 feet away from us, while the second monkey landed on the other side of a huge boulder in the middle of the stream. Neither animal had screamed or struggled, but had fallen directly downward without hitting any of the foliage.

I immediately climbed around the detour we had just past and back down to the stream where the monkey had fallen. Nothing. I searched along the stream and on the stream bank for more than an hour, and Johnson and his assistant also came down to help, but we never were able to find the second monkey. We finally assumed that it had been able to scramble away through the vegetation. But one specimen was better than none at all. And on closer inspection of our specimen, we found it to be a small black monkey, about 24 inches in length from its head to the base of the tail, with cream-colored hair on its face, chest and upper arms.

The next day, Mr. Graff collected a second monkey on the far end of the island, as well as an agouti that had never before been recorded. Rats, however, were reasonably common, and he trapped several near the deserted bungalow, and he captured a large golden brown rat in the hills.

Assisting with the trapping of the rats near the bungalow, we found that it was necessary to remain on-site all night. If we left out baited traps at dusk and returned the following morning, we found that all the traps had caught rats, but little more remained than feet and bits of hair. Some predator or other rats made fast work of the trapped animals. By remaining on-site, however, retrieving and preparing each fresh specimen soon after it was trapped, we were able to take all of the specimens necessary during the first half of one night.

Also during our stay at Gorgona, the expedition archeologist, Mr. Camp, discovered some curious carved stones at numerous sites above the beach. He took several of us to see a sample of his carved stones one afternoon, and they indeed were fascinating. One was a carved monkey with a stiff tail arched over the back, but with a bird's head and strongly curved beak, like that of a flamingo. Another rock contained two human figures standing side be side, with strange grooves radiating out from their heads, forming a halo, straight legs, and out-turned feet. On their right arms were coils of some sort, with one end turning upward to pass into the rays of their halos. We dubbed these figures as "Adam and Eve."

During the course of Mr. Camp's nine-day survey of Gorgona, he found dozens of carved rocks. Many were of ancient designs, but others were more recent. There was one with a three-masted ship, judged to date from the first half of the last century. The most modern of these contained the name and date. "F. D'Croz, 1847" was deeply incised upon it. We later learned that D. Croz had once leased the island.

During the final days on Gorgona, once Ms. Clouster had collected a great number of specimens and was spending the majority of her time in preserving specimens, I was totally on my own. Although I remained on her beckon-call when aboard ship, it seemed that she preferred to work alone, unlike Major Johnson and Mr. Graff, who invited my help with preparing skins continuously.

Finally, on July 20, 1924, we set sail for the Galapagos Islands, a thousand miles west of Gorgona and about 600 miles off the coast of Ecuador. From a distance, the Galapagos appeared mysterious and foreboding. They gave off a yellowish hue, due, I later discovered, to the reduced foliage that was more like tiny scales than ordinary leaves.

I was eager to experience the Galapagos because I had read about how these islands were responsible for Charles Darwin's theory of evolution. It was the wildlife on the Galapagos, especially the varied finches that had finally convinced Darwin that natural selection was the principal cause of speciation.

Discussions about evolution were commonplace among the expedition scientists, and I found myself listening to each intently. Never before had I learned so much about such things, and the conversations about natural selection were one of the most exciting of all. I had been raised in a Christian setting that rarely addressed the idea of evolution. But, suddenly, here I was in the midst of Darwin's crucible of information.

We found a wonderland of animals on the Galapagos, each species so tame that they would allow us to approach within inches. Although many of the animals we encountered had no common name, most of the species could easily be identified to family or sometimes genus. Dark blue herons were commonplace along the shoreline, and a pair of oystercatchers, with scarlet legs and bright yellow legs, greeted us each time we landed on James Island. A unique cormorant was found in Tagus Cove and on nearby Marborough Island.

Vermillion flycatchers, a brilliant red and black bird, were one of our favorite little birds, although the much larger, stately scarlet flamingo was another favorite. And we also saw several broad-winged hawks, doves, and strange looking mockingbirds, all species that Major Johnson claimed were unique to these islands.

Seabirds were also of special interest. Fork-tailed gulls were commonplace. Huge albatrosses and storm-petrels were seen on numerous occasions. Gannets circled overhead throughout the day, and we watched as they would suddenly drop like a stone into the water, where they became completely submerged for a few seconds, before rising again with a fish they had caught. And brown pelicans were commonplace as well.

We found a number of pelican nests, and were able to approach within a few inches before they would flap away to a perch on an adjacent rock. Many of their nests contained eggs, but in late July, none contained nestlings. However, Major Johnson found a blue-footed booby with a single chick on the floor of Daphe Crater; he collected both.

Mr. Graff was especially delighted with the friendly sea-lions, who often came out of the water to waddle up close for a better examination of the strange invaders. We were even able to approach the young sea-lions, although the mothers seemed uneasy when we approached their youngsters too close. And while swimming in the coves, one or more of these marvelous creatures would often accompany me. Their swimming ability far surpassed my capability, even though I had been swimming in salt water all my life. Each day we swam at least every evening, since fresh water was at a minimum. And with each swim I found it surprising to find the water so cool, not at all like most equatorial waters.

All the while we were present in the Galapagos, we searched for the huge tortoises that Darwin and others had written about. We did find an occasional track or, once, marks of their scales in a sheltered place under a huge volcanic rock. And finally, on Albemarle Island, our herpetologist, Mr. Cutter, discovered hundreds of shells of the giant tortoises. The great reptiles had all been killed with machete blows. Mr. Cutter later explained that native Ecuadorians killed them for their oil, a product that can be sold in Guayaquil for about nine dollars for 100 pounds.

"It is possible," he said, "that this magnificent endemic species will soon disappear, like the extinct dodo. Darwin found the species abundant; he recorded thousands on these islands. Since they do not have any natural predators, they apparently have been all but wiped out for their oil or by sailors for food. It is a sad statement of things to come."

At the time, I gave his prophetic words little heed, as it seemed to me that the Galapagos were full of wildlife of every kind imaginable. But I never forgot those words, and in time I was to agree completely with these sentiments.

In spite of the significant decline of tortoises, another large reptile, a marine lizard, was abundant. These huge sluggish iguanas possessed a crest running from their head to their tail, and a blunt snout. We all called them "amblies," after their scientific names, *Amblyrhynchus crissatus*. They were amazing creatures that, instead of eating insects and other small creatures on land, they fed on seaweed some distance from shore. They would swim out several hundred yards from a perch on the black rocks, which they seemed to prefer when on shore, and actually would dive beneath the waves to browse on the abundant seaweed growing on the off-shore rocks. Then they would return to a favorite perch and bask on the black rocks in the hot sun until it was again lunchtime.

Darwin had taken a great interest in these marine lizards and pointed out that, in spite of their habit of feeding underwater, they could not be forced into the sea, but would cower on the rocks. We confirmed this for ourselves by herding them to the edge of the cliff where they not only would not take the plunge into the sea, but they crouched down with absolutely no defense. We actually picked some up and threw them into the sea, where they immediately swam back to the shore and clamored back onto the rocks. Darwin had suggested that this peculiarity may have been inherited from a time when these lizards were not marine animals.

Another interesting life form of the rocky shoreline was a huge red and blue crab that often basked on the rocks by the hundreds. And unlike most crabs, they too hesitated to go into the water, but would run about on the lava rocks when approached.

It was while I was attempting to collect some of these crabs for our supper that I discovered a number of large crayfish hiding just off-shore under rocks. These marvelous creatures soon became a favorite. We found that they hid under shelving rocks with only their long antennae visible, gentle waving in the water. The sailors got very good at grabbing them and pulling them out of their retreat. Those 12- to 18-inch-long creatures made excellent eating.

As might be expected on an island with so many unique creatures, the insect life was also worthy of collecting. And Ms. Clouster and I made numerous trips to various parts of each island we visited for the express purpose of collecting new and unusual species. We would return from each sojourn with several specimens, many of which she believed had never before been collected. I recall only two of those to any extent, and one was a spider, not an insect.

I was first attracted to odd spiderwebs stretched between some of the black lava rocks. And on closer examination we found spiders that looked very much like a cross between a crab and a garden spider, with black-and-yellow patterns and scarlet markings. And in the same habitat were black-and-yellow locust, measuring almost four inches from wing tip to wing tip. I wondered if the inch-long spiders preyed on the larger locust.

All my life I had an aversion to spiders, and so when Ms. Clouster ordered me to collect several, I approached each one very cautiously. I guess I half expected them to jump at me, but they were extremely sluggish, not at all like many of the spiders I was familiar with. Each one collected seemed less frightening, although I made sure that I had a secure hold with my tweezers before placing it into the jar of alcohol.

It finally came time to leave the Galapagos, and I was very ready to continue our travels. So it was a real disappointment when I learned that we were going to return to Panama for additional supplies before we headed west across the Pacific to the Marquesas.

Our trip back to Panama went very well, as the winds were favorable throughout. We anchored again off Balboa on the last day of August 1925. We remained in port for only four days, during which time I again helped with the purchase of supplies. I also cabled my mother and stepfather about my plans to continue on with the expedition, and twice I attempted to find Beaman, but without success. He had mailed specimens the week before we had arrived, and was expected again in a few days. But the *St. Maria* sailed before he returned.

Chapter 4

At long last we were off across the Pacific, the longest ocean trip of our voyage. We sailed the approximately 3,000 miles in nearly six weeks. What a sensation it was to realize that our route was taking us across the most extensive ocean-crossing in the world. This topic, of course, became a point of discussion among the scientists. Opinions differed between the route from Australia to Cape Horn and the region in which we were now sailing, but most sided with our current crossing. At about the half-way point, Colonel Spencer, our marine biologist, stated: "Here we are," he said, "1,500 miles north of the Galapagos. Australia is nearly 6,000 miles to the west, the Clipperton Atoll is about 1,000 miles to the northeast, and the Marquesas lie 1,500 miles ahead."

Never before had I wondered about the immense size of the ocean. Our ship seemed like a tiny cork, bobbing along with its cargo of humanity. We did not see another human being, other than our crew, for the entire voyage. We did, however, pick up a few radio broadcasts, mainly from San Francisco, but occasionally also from Nebraska and Boston. It was strange to realize that we were listening to news, and once, a live concert taking place in cities so very far away. It was like we were eavesdropping on a completely different world. I felt very much alone.

At times during those six weeks, memories of home and my brief love affair with Suzana haunted me. Although I had experienced a few sexual encounters before Suzana during my early teen years on St. Croix, I had never before experienced love. Those first times had been little more than passion, but I had made love to Suzana. What a difference! And I dreamed of falling in love again.

Most thoughts of home, however, primarily evolved around various excursions with my stepfather - hunting deer at East End, exploring Krause Lagoon or Salt River Bay, and climbing Eagle Mountain - or swimming in the island streams or fishing on the pier at Fredericksted.

Henny and I talked about our homes on numerous occasions. But, while his memories, while growing up in Baltimore and being thrown out of his house by a drunken stepfather, were mostly unpleasant and sad, mine were almost always happy ones. For that reason, I suppose, Henny asked me about my upbringing whenever the opportunity arose.

"Greg," he would say, "whod is hap'non on your St. Croix, today?" And his question would immediately bring to mind some adventure. I realized then that my growing up years on St. Croix, such a tiny speck of land in the vast Caribbean Sea, was all that a boy could want.

"Fall migrants arrive in October," I told him one day. "And the arrival of the golden plovers was the highlight of the fall season. Those fat, juicy birds are present on our island for only a short time, before they continued on through the Antilles to their wintering grounds in Argentina, and that several of the men would arrange a great shoot. One of my earliest memories was accompanying my stepfather on the annual plover hunts."

"I've 'ner eaten plovers. Who'd the taste like," Henny asked. "Wonderful sweet taste," I answered. "They are very different than any other wild game. Much better than dove. Like chicken, I suppose, but with a wild, tangy taste." After a slight pause, I added: "I suppose that their taste comes from the abundant berries on their tundra breeding grounds. They gorge themselves in preparation for their long journey. St. Croix is but one of several essential stops, where they rest and replenish their energy, along their route."

"On one hunt, three years ago, Barney James, one of my stepfather's friends, had a terrible accident. He actually blew his chin off. We found him walking across the pasture, holding his chin and completely covered with blood. It was a terrible scene."

"Did he live," Henny asked. "Yes, he did, but he came very close to dying before we got him to a hospital. After he recovered, he grew a huge, bushy mustache and beard to hide what little was left of his chin."

At another time, I explained that October is cane-planting time on the islands. "St. Croix has plenty of the two ingredients necessary for growing sugar cane, fertile soil and plenty rain. During October, the entire island becomes bright green with the new cane crop." After a few seconds, I added: "My island is truly a garden. No place on earth is so green and lovely. Every October, the island's plains and rolling hills become green with fresh cane."

Henny was more interested in the rum, a product of sugar cane, than my descriptions of the island. He asked me once, "Tell me how rum is made from the cane? Tis it crushed like grapes?"

"In a way," I answered. "Pieces of cane are ground up and crushed in mills powered either by the wind or steam. St. Croix has dozens of windmills, scattered all over the island." I couldn't help but think about the picturesque, rock mills of my homeland, and I actually got a little misty. "The juice is hauled off to distilleries, where it is first fermented before distilling. My stepfather, Mr. Kristof, says that St. Croix's sugar cane makes the world's best rum. He should know, because he is the manager of the largest rum plant on St. Croix. They use a secret Dutch recipe that was brought to St. Croix in the early 1600s."

"Greg, did ye taste the rum from St. Croix often?" Henny asked, as if he expected me to be a connoisseur. "Rarely," I said, "and I never drank it straight. I much preferred rum cocktails made from limes, sugar water, and rum. My mother warned me about drinking straight rum. She told me that rum was addictive, and warned me to stay away from the spirits." And then, from the blue, I remembered an old rhyme, that I recited:

"This happy beverage, joy inspiring bowl,
 Dispelling far the shades of mental night,
 Wakes bright ideas on the raptur'd soul,

And sorrow turns to pleasure and delight."

Henny laughed and said that he agreed with that. "From my experience we'd rum, 'tis given me much pleasure and delight. Aye, with ladies of the night." And after a brief pause, he added, "How I wish right now we had a jug of rum and two Panama ladies."

Most of the scientists kept pretty much together during the crossing, rarely talking with the sailors. My status was somewhere in the middle, not really part of either group, but somewhat accepted by both. My friend Henny was well liked by all the sailors, and so I was at least tolerated by that quarter. And because of my ability to help with specimen preparation, I was also accepted by the scientists.

I became most friendly with Mr. Johnson, who seemed genuinely interested in me and my knowledge of the West Indies. He mentioned several times that someday he hoped to visit all the Caribbean islands, and he asked me many questions about the Virgin Islands and Puerto Rico. Although I had only casual knowledge about Puerto Rico's bird life, I was reasonably aware of all the species to be found in the Virgin Islands.

Mr. Johnson seemed very interested in the winter birds, those that nest in North America and migrate to the West Indies for the winter months. He was especially interested in the habitats utilized by the wintering songbirds. "Do wintering warblers utilize the mangroves forests or only the forest habitats?" he asked. "I've found warblers in both habitats, and they are especially common in the vegetation along the freshwater streams," I answered. "One of my favorite warbler areas is Caledonia Gut, where there is a mountain stream that drains into Hams Bay. A day's hike through Caledonia is likely to produce all the wintering songbirds possible on St. Croix."

He was even interested in knowing what species could be expected. And so I tried to give him a rough list in some sort of priority order: "Black-and-white, parula, prairie, black-throated green, hooded, Cape May, worm-eating, magnolia, and hooded warblers, and ovenbird and American redstart are most numerous" I said. Then I added, "Blackpolls are common very briefly in the fall. But I have also found myrtle, black-throated blue, Kentucky, blue-winged, and even Connecticut warblers. And once I found a Maryland yellowthroat. Northern waterthrushes are most numerous in the mangroves."

He looked at me with what I assumed to be admiration, and said, "Mr. Stewart, you know your birds. Someday, I want you to take me to Caledonia Gut so I can see for myself." I told him that I would be honored to do so.

Ms. Clouster seldom spent any time with the other scientists; most of her time aboard ship was spent in her cabin. I suppose she read and studied her specimens. She did invite me in once during the crossing. She apparently had completed her labeling and pinning the specimens, and she seemed anxious to show her handiwork to someone. Either she thought that I would be the most interested, or I possessed the least threat, I wasn't sure. And so I spent about two hours with her one evening after supper. She went from specimen to specimen, telling me all she knew about each. I was much impressed, and I acted totally interested in all that she had to say.

She finally finished her lecture, and after two or three polite questions, I was excused. She had very neatly mounted all of her more than 400 specimens on pins, each with a tiny label on which she had included the location and date of collection, all positioned in rows in about two dozen cedar boxes. An additional 100 or more empty boxes, stacked in one corner, awaited additional specimens.

Suppertime seemed to be one of the few times that all of the scientists and their helpers, myself included, spent any time together. We ate each evening with the captain, who was a very friendly sort, and also curious about how he could best serve the scientists. I was able to learn more about the voyage on these occasions than at any other time.

The plan for the expedition, I learned, was to visit several of the island-groups within the area commonly referred to as "Polynesia." Although some of these islands had previously been visited by other scientific expeditions, many of our stops were scheduled on little known islands. Mr. Johnson explained one purpose for the variety of stops: "Although all the principal islands are mountainous, the result of dramatic volcanic activity thousands of years ago, the Marquesas Islands are all tropical. But Tahiti, like the Hawaiian Islands to the north, actually possesses montane elements. And Easter Island may best represent the lower islands."

"Do you expect to find more animals and plants on Tahiti, because of the wider variety of habitats?" I asked Mr. Johnson. He answered, "Yes and no. Although each habitat will support its own set of species, we are more likely to find the greatest number of species on the larger islands. Particularly those that possess extensive forest."

"Yes, indeed," said Mr. Graff, "but one must also realize how depauperate of flora and fauna oceanic islands are. They are far from the continents where the species were originally derived. In fact, many kinds of plants and animals, such as mammals, snakes, lizards, and even conifers, never reach these islands.

But the species that did make it were all likely to find vacant niches in which they could fill. Like Darwin's finches on the Galapagos, they may quickly - perhaps in a few hundred generations - actually evolve into complete new species. That is one of our interests. To find new species."

"But how will you recognize a new species? Especially when you have nothing to compare it with,?" I asked. Ms. Clouster answered for the first time: "In the case of insects, species that reproduce very quickly, compared with birds or plants, it is very difficult," she said. Then she added: "That is why our collections are so important. More often than not with insects, we will not be certain until we return to England and are able to compare them with previously collected specimens at our own museums and at a few other museums with representative families in other countries."

Mr. Graff next turned to Professor Cornell, the geologist. "Dr. Cornell, do you expect to discover new rocks?"

Cornell chuckled, and then very seriously responded: "That actually is a possibility. But my major interest is land forms, especially those derived from coral. I want to learn more about how the coral islands evolve."

Mr. Spencer went on to explain how coral reefs develop in warm, shallow seas, and gradually form an atoll. Eventually an island begins to build within the center.

"I intend to establish a timeframe by which such phenomena occur," added Cornell.

"There is an additional purpose for our expedition," Johnson added. "I am especially interested in documenting specific populations of island species."

"Indeed," said Dr. Kagan and Mr. Nichols almost as one. Nichols continued, "Man's various activities on all the oceanic islands have already eliminated both plants and animals wherever he has gone. This is especially true on islands."

Mr. Johnson added: "Nine-tenth of all bird extinctions have occurred on islands, which have a combined land-mass of only one-fifth the world's total land mass. Since the year 1600, when the first written records of such things began, we know of at least 170 extinctions. More than 150 of those are island forms. That's more than ninety percent." He paused as if to let those figures sink in. Then he added "I hope that this expedition can document additional details about species numbers as well as new species."

Everyone there that evening was looking forward to our explorations, and that discussion between the scientists seemed to help me better understand the purpose of our expedition.

At times on our long voyage across the South Pacific, we found that we were not alone. Dolphins and whales were seen on several occasions. It was always a treat to find these mammals of the sea, and I attempted to identify each one. We were able to identify six dolphins: common, Gray's, spinner, striped, bridled, and bottle-nosed. Common dolphins were present much of the time, often swimming along the bow. And on several occasions, as I watched them in admiration, one or more would roll over on its side and look up at me as if it were as curious about me as I was about it.

Spinner dolphins were also fairly common, and always in large schools of 20 to 100 individuals. But they never came close to the ship. Sometimes, when we suddenly came upon a school, they would scatter in all directions, churning the water into a boiling foam with their rapid retreat.

Mr. Graff pointed out that the bridled porpoises were surface feeders that preyed on flying-fish. And so it became great fun to watch these seven-foot porpoises in hot pursuit of a 12-inch flying fish. The porpoise's speed and agility was a thing to behold.

The whales mostly remained just far enough away so that we never were able to see them very well. Mr. Graff identified seven whale species in all during our crossing: fin, blue, piked, sei, tropical, sperm, and pilot whales. The largest of these, up to 100 feet long, was the blue whale that we saw on several occasions. Its long and streamlined body, with a tiny fin set far back of the blow hole, and its blue-gray color, mottled with light gray and white, help to identify this mammoth creature. For the most part, the blue whales were extremely shy.

Fin whales, however, sometimes came much closer, and I was able to study this huge creature for long periods of time. Their color pattern of a blue-black back and white underparts was obvious, and they had a rather distinct breathing and diving sequence. They would emit a single blow about 20 feet high that widened at its apex, followed by a long, slow, and fairly shallow roll, repeated four or five times at intervals of 10 to 20 seconds. Henny and I even were able to time its dives. Some individuals could remain down for up to 20 minutes.

But the pilot whales were the most interesting. Pods of 30 to 35 individuals were recorded on numerous occasions, and they seemed oblivious to our presence. Encountering a traveling pod, they simply dipped under the bow and continued on their way. We often could detect their presence by their staccato popping sounds. Their behavior was so predictable that Major Douglas decided that he would attempt to collect one of these 18- to 22-foot-long cetaceans. So when we next met a pod, he shot one of the smaller individuals. But his one shot did not kill it outright, and it dove underwater to escape. We immediately doubled back as best we could, and began to search for the badly wounded whale.

It was then, during our search, that we discovered two other pilot whales, one on each side of our prey, holding it up and escorting it out of harm's way. They even submerged with their injured companion, as if attempting to elude us, but were forced to resurface every 10 to 15 minutes to breathe. If wasn't until Mr. Graff fired a second bullet into the wounded whale, totally incapacitating it from any further escape, before its two companions submerged and left the scene.

Never before had I seen such compassion among wildlife as I had with the two pilot whales' attempt to save their fellow being. It also was an act of bravery that few humans would be capable of providing. All of us were greatly moved. Since then I have developed great respect and admiration for whales and their fellow cetaceans.

Retrieving the dead whale required heavy ropes and pulleys to get it on the deck. And preparing the huge specimen took us several days. The abundant fatty tissues had to be totally removed before the skin could be salted for preservation. The entire skeleton was cleaned, as well. It was a nasty job.

Birds were reasonably common in mid-ocean, although we might go for a good part of a day without seeing a single individual. Then suddenly we would find ourselves amidst a flock of several dozen to several hundred individuals. Petrels and shearwaters were most numerous, flying rapidly over the surface of the water, skimming over the crests and disappearing in the troughs. Sooner or later one of these pelagics would approach close enough for a shot. More often than not, however, they would beat to and fro across the stern or circle the ship at some distance. Kermedec, Herald, white-necked, Cook's, and Bulwer's petrels, as well wedge-tailed, short-tailed, and Christmas shearwaters were all collected during the voyage.

We also saw an occasional tropicbirds and one lone booby. Mr. Johnson managed to collect one of the tropicbirds, a red-tailed tropicbird, that flew close to the ship. It was a marvelous creature with a red bill and long, red tail streamers. It's pure white plumage, except for narrow black streaks on it's wings and tail, gave it a very clean appearance. These pelagic birds spend all their lives at sea, except for short nesting periods on several of the South Pacific islands. Mr. Johnson explained that they rest on the ocean's surface at night.

On another occasion an adult masked booby landed on our deck, and waddled about as if it thought the *St. Maria* was an island. It, too, was collected, and I had the privilege of preparing the skin. It was a large, streamlined bird with an all-white head and back and black face, tail, and along the trailing edge of its otherwise snow-white wings. After completing the study skin, I examined the stomach contents and discovered several species of small fish that Mr. Spencer immediately preserved for later identification.

Fish were surprisingly uncommon in mid-ocean, although they were numerous nearer the continent. Although we managed to hook an occasional bonito, albacore, and coryphaena, the only fish species that seemed commonplace was the flying-fish. We found this pelagic species quite tasty, although a little dry. And we had great sport in watching these amazing creatures glide long distances over the waves. Some may have covered a good 50 yards, and some even bounced off rising waves that gave extra impetus to their flights.

It took us 40 days to reach the southern group of the Marquesas. And on out first sight of land, the large island of Hiva Oa, we all gave great cheers for our safe arrival. Although dark clouds hung from the rocky, black peaks, bright shafts of sunlight highlighted several patches of greenery along the shore. Clusters of mango trees dotted the lower slopes and coconut palms and screw pines lined the bays. As we came along Cape Balguerie, the island's southeastern point, we searched the shore for our first signs of habitation.

It took us some time before we discovered the narrow entrance to Ta-hu-ku, or the Bay of Traitors, that provided a natural harbor with sandy beaches and a palm-studded valley beyond. And as we moved to our anchorage, the beach became lined with natives. The women wore loose cotton dresses and stiff straw hats adorned with a bright ribbon or handkerchief, while the men all wore white shirts and either khaki or blue dungaree trousers. They made a colorful welcoming committee.

Within the hour, the island's Administrator came aboard to inspect our papers. And once he was satisfied that we were legal visitors, he left with a promise that he would return the next morning for an official welcome.

Although we were all anxious to go ashore, the evening past quickly with much talk about our hopes for the next several days. The scientists talked principally about what they planned to accomplish, but the sailors had other things in mind. And I admit that the appearance of the young ladies lining the shore created urges that I had put aside during our crossing.

Our location in Atuona Bay was marvelous. Mt. Temetiu, approximately 3,000 feet elevation, provided a harsh but ideal backdrop to the lush valley. And with the setting sun, the surrounding clouds turned bright pink, contrasting with the heavier, black clouds hanging below the rocky peaks.

Chapter 5

We did not go ashore until after lunch. The French Governor and his Commissaries, or police chief and staff, came aboard during the morning, and Captain Bonney politely escorted them on a complete tour of our ship. Although many of us had begun to take her for granted, she was one of the finest three-masted barkentines ever built. And it was obvious that the governor and his colleagues had great appreciation of her construction and appearance. The *St. Maria* was, indeed, a beautiful ship. Built as a yacht in 1890, she was 191 feet in length, with a beam of 32 feet, and an inner hull of iron encased in a sheathing of steel.

By the time our group of scientists finally went ashore, we had only time enough to walk the length of the valley before returning to the ship. But what an enchanting valley it was. The floor of Atuona Valley was filled with coconut palms, mangoes, breadfruit, bananas, and various other trees. Beneath those trees were a scattering of wood houses, each on a rock base. Almost a mile up the valley was the French headquarters for the Marquesas Islands. This complex consisted of a series of larger, better built structures that served as the offices and residents for the Governor and his staff. The well-maintained yards, more like European gardens, that surrounded the buildings, contained a variety of other plants, including perfumed frangipani and graceful kapok trees, and an abundance of scarlet hibiscus and white jasmine shrubs.

The people we encountered on our walk that afternoon were some of the friendliest I had ever met anywhere. All dressed in their conventional garb, they greeted each of us with great smiles and much laughter. And yet, the ancestors of these people had practiced cannibalism only a generation or two before.

42

Also during our walk we stopped to admire the large stone Roman Catholic Church, just back from the main street. It was constructed of coral rock with a fresh coating of whitewash, and it possessed a tall steeple with a huge copper bell. We were warmly greeted by the Bishop, Monsignor Antonio, who we learned had spent 24 years at Atuona. He seemed perfectly happy with his place in life.

The Monsignor insisted on showing us the church and the adjacent school house and other buildings. He also introduced us to a number of his staff, including a young lady he called "Katrina." Maybe because I was the only one of our group that was close to her age, she watched me all during our visit. And I could hardly take my eyes off her. She had a lovely body and golden brown skin, and her wonderfully dark eyes seemed to stare deep into my soul.

That evening I told Henny that I had met the girl of my dreams. He made fun of me. "Greg, my friend," he said, "you'll find ye be in love on every island we visit." Then he stopped, looked me over as if to make a pronouncement, and said, "You are a romantic. But for me," he added, "love is one island after de other."

He also told me that two of the sailors had swam to shore the previous night and had no trouble at all finding "two beautiful maidens" willing to share their beds. He warned me, "The captain might not take favorable to one of his crew takin' in we's one of the Bishop's girls." I fell asleep that night with Katrina on my mind.

Morning dawned with all its glory, and our first full day on Hiva Oa had begun. Arrangements had been made the previous day to hire a horse-drawn wagon to haul the scientists and all our gear up the valley and onto the upper plateau, to where we could camp. Passing the church, I searched for Katrina, but was disappointed in not seeing her. She undoubtedly was busy with whatever her work entailed.

Not far beyond where we had all turned back the previous day, we came to an old cemetery, where we stopped. The higher ground provided a marvelous view of the valley and bay. And when our driver, Darnano, motioned for us to follow him, we climbed out of the wagon and walked into the very neat and picturesque cemetery. There among the numerous graves was that of Paul Gauguin, the famous French painter. Darnano explained that Gauguin had moved to Atuona in 1901, had taken up with a 14-year-old mistress named Vaeoho, and had died a year later at the age of 55. "When Tioka, Gauguin's neighbor, found him dead in bed, Darnano explained, in broken English,

"Tioka he de head, a Marquesan custom to find he really dead. Den no doubt. He den cried 'Ua mate Koke!" and he ran tell de commissar."

Darnano also told us that Gauguin had constantly been in conflict with the island's colonial authorities. "Just de week fore he dead," he said, "Gauguin convicted of libel of a gendarme, and he bin sentence to three mons prison. He not a nice person; I saw he once when I was boy."

When we topped over the rim onto the plateau, where the road ended, we could see all of the southern and eastern half of the island. What an incredible view! Our photographer, Mr. Ashley, took several photographs. A view down Atuona Valley, into Traitor's Bay and the varied colored water beyond, presented us with a truly enchanting scene. Beyond, we could see the islands of Mohotani and Fato Hiva, and as clear a day as it was, I imagined I could see all the way to Easter Island, a couple thousand miles to the east. Closer, the tall steeple of the Atuona church was easily visible in the green valley below. I thought of Katrina, and wondered if she was also thinking of me.

Nearby was a marvelous forest, and my entire attention was soon focused on that lush new world. After making camp in a lovely glade just inside the forest, we followed a narrow path through the forest that gradually increased in elevation. It took us a good part of two hours before we reached the lip of the next plateau. While the lower plateau possessed some evidence of cleared plots for gardens, the higher plateau seemed untouched.

I later learned that most of the island's lowland forest had been striped by sandalwood traders of all the sandalwood shrubs they could find. In the process they had damaged much of the native forest. Sandalwood could then be found only in remote, difficult to reach areas of the island. Sandalwood had a fragrance much in demand in China, where its oils were made into perfumes and medicines.

The higher plateau was delightfully cool. The lower valley had been quite warm the previous afternoon, but the upper forest was marvelous. This was the area with the greatest diversity of plants and wildlife that was most likely to produce the greatest number of unique species. So we set out in various parties to see what we might discover.

Ms. Clouster, with me in tow, continued straight ahead on the path through the forest. The ground-cover was often dominated by huge bracken ferns that reminded me very much of the swamp ferns that occur in moist places in the Virgin Islands. But there also were extensive areas with little undergrowth. We stopped every now and then, each time we came to a slightly different environment, to collect whatever insect species might be present. It was an extremely successful day, Ms. Clouster told me afterwards. We had collected more than 600 individual insects on the upper plateau. Most impressive of these were the amazing variety of butterflies and huge armored beetles.

The bird and mammal collections, on the other hand, were rather disappointing, according to Mr. Graff and Mr. Johnson. Mr. Graff had collected only a few rats, and Mr. Johnson had taken less than a dozen bird species.

The next day on the upper plateau was a repeat of the first, but in reverse order. After a full morning of collecting, we folded camp and began our slow descent into Atuona Valley. The next day was New Years Eve, and all the scientists had been invited to the Governor's house for a party. I, for one, looked forward to such an occasion, and also the possibility that I might again meet Katrina.

It was a wonderful party with plenty of drink and a dinner that I will long remember. Roasted pig was the highlight; it was delicious! Never before had I eaten such wonderful pork. The additional foods included various seafoods, a local crayfish, yams, fried bananas in a sweet sauce, and a number of other wonderful tasty foods. All were extraordinary. But the pork was the best tasting meat I have ever experienced.

Monsignor Antonio was also present, and I so wanted to ask the Monsignor about Katrina, but the opportunity never arose. There was considerable toasting before, during, and after the meal. It seemed to me that the dozen or so locals in attendance were searching for whatever excuse they could find for an additional toast.

After the initial very proper toasts, for our safe arrival, the expedition's success, our continued success, and the memory of a past Governor, that apparently had died in office only a couple years earlier, the toasts took on a different perspective. And later I wrote down some of these, and used them on various occasions thereafter. Those that appealed to me most included the following, although I can no longer which of the guests was responsible.

> "To our host, an excellent man,
> For is not a man fully judged by the company he keeps."
> and
> "Here's a toast to all who are here,
> No matter where you're from;

May the best day you've seen
Be worse than you're worst to come."
   and
"Health to my body, wealth to my purse,
Heaven to my soul, and I wish you no worse."
   and
"Here's to those who love us,
And here's to those who don't;
A smile for those who are willing to,
And a tear for those who won't."

By the time midnight and the new year arrived, most of the guests, as well as the Governor and Monsignor Antonio, had reached a high level of intoxication.

It was almost 2 p.m. before we left the Governor's party. We undoubtedly made a noisy and hilarious troupe as we made our way back to the beach where our boat was tied. But approaching the beach, we found an even wilder party underway. As many as 50 to 60 people were dancing around a huge bonfire. Several of our sailors mingled with the half-clad natives. They all were drinking rum. A small band of drummers kept up a steady and rather provocative beat that seemed to heighten the excitement. We naturally joined in the partying, and we soon found ourselves absorbed in the strange drum beat.

Not being as intoxicated as most of my shipmates, I soon found a huge log along the edge of the clearing and sat down to watch the partiers. The dancing reminded me very much of the provocative gestations of the native Virgin Islanders. Henny was one of the dancers. He had found a shapely native girl who was one of the dancers who was teaching him their peculiar style of dancing. He put on quite a show, and his unique dance became a topic of discussion for all the remainder of our voyage. It was obvious that none of the native people possessed any inhibitions, as most of the women had shed whatever dress they had worn at the start of the night. Most wore only a throng that hung from their waist in a wonderfully provocative manner.

Suddenly, without warning, Katrina was at my side. She grabbed my hand and asked me to dance. I had not seen her before, although I had searched for her among the dancers. She also wore only a loose throng, and I could hardly believe that she was here, and had come to my side. I was actually tongue-tied, and could barely look at her beautiful body. What extraordinary breasts she possessed. But I was soon swaying to the temptacious beat of the drums.

I saw Henny only once while dancing, and when I looked for him a short time later, he and his friend had left the party. In fact, many of the couples, including most of the sailors, had disappeared. So, when Katrina took my hand and guided me away, it seemed only logical. We walked, arm and arm, to one of the tiny wood houses. And within a very few minutes we were making love.

Katrina was an amazing lover. It was obvious that she knew all about the ways to satisfy a man. I experienced a marvelous night. And when she awoke me at dawn, we again made love against the sounds of the dawn chorus of birds. Afterwards, we walked together to the beach, where we held each other as the surf caressed our bodies. Then she kissed me goodbye and walked up the beach and out of my life.

The entire affair seemed so natural that, later, I could not help but wonder about her total lack of inhibitions. And from a later conversation with Henny, many of the sailors told of similar experiences. I must admit that, although I had totally enjoyed our lovemaking, it lacked the romance that I had desired. And oddly enough, I never saw her again.

We remained in port for only one more day, and that was spent exploring the slopes of Temetiu. From the deck of the *St. Maria*, I had noticed a zigzag path leading up the steep slope, on the left side of the valley. And when I suggested this route as a way to sample another habitat, Mr. Johnson, Mr. Graff, and Mr. Nichols, our botanist, agreed that it would be worthwhile. Ms. Clouster decided to remain on board, but she asked me to collect whatever new insects I might find.

The trail was steep and rough, with segments badly eroded from heavy rains that had ran down the trail like an open ditch. The entire distance from the village to the ridge was less than one mile, but the zigzag route was at least twice that. Near the top, the cliffs formed a great amphitheatre, and it was there where a dozen or more of the pure white terns were soaring. Although we had seen several of these little seabirds fishing over the bay, they had stayed at a distance, and Mr. Johnson had been unable to obtain one. But there in the amphitheatre, he was able to shoot two individuals with little difficulty. And on climbing down the steep slope, through the tangle of shrubs and small trees to retrieve one of the birds, I discovered one of the white terns sitting on a bare branch that held a single egg.

After retrieving the dead tern, I climbed the little tree to collect the egg that was perfectly balanced on the open branch. The setting tern flew off when I approached, and it made several dives at me until I departed. It was a remarkable bird with pure white plumage and coal black eyes and bill.

The next day, Mr. Johnson told me that the white terns he had shot that day represented a smaller and different species – the Marquesan white tern – than the other all-white terns we had seen and collected along the shore.

"I must collect several more of the endemic forms," he said. "They will make excellent specimens that I can use in trades for other specimens for our museum." Although I did not question him at the time, I did wonder at the appropriateness of taking large numbers of a relatively rare species that was restricted to a single island.

One of the most remarkable finds during the day was a little valley, just below the peak, that was totally filled with blue forget-me-nots. Mr. Nichols was greatly impressed and collected several samples. We thereafter dubbed that place as "forget-me-not valley."

Just beyond the valley, at the base of a cliff, we discovered a little trough that had been cut into the cliff that produced a little waterfall. And at the base of the waterfall was a myriad of ferns and other plants. Mr. Nichols identified a dozen species of ferns and a gigantic hart's-tongue with leaves five feet long and a foot across.

Also present near the base of the waterfall was a lone tiki, standing alone under a huge mango tree. The tiki was badly weathered, but we were able to copy the design to show Mr. Camp after returning to the ship. Mr. Camp was much impressed by the design, and stated that "Of the two dozen or more tikis I have examined on the island, none are as elaborate as this one. This one may be very special. I really must see it for myself."

Tikis, I learned, were the stone gods of the early Polynesians. Although they were no longer worshiped as they were before Christianity was introduced to the islands, they are still held in high esteem. And Mr. Camp said that a few of the older Marquesans still believe in their power.

Since our next stop on our journey was at Hanalapa, on the north side of Hiva Oa, plans were made for Mr. Johnson, Mr. Camp, Mr. Ashley, and I to hike across the mountain, past the unusual tiki. We were to meet the *St. Maria* at Hanamenu, a village along the northern coast not far from Hanalapa.

The next day's hike to the waterfall began without incident. Mr. Johnson collected eight of the white terns, and Mr. Ashley was able to photograph the tiki from numerous angles. However, we encountered heavy rain on the northern slope, and the trail became a muddy and dangerous undertaking. I had brought along a pack with several collecting jars, and several of these valuable containers were broken in falls on the slippery trail by the time we reached the lower forest. I was later soundly chastised by Ms. Clouster for my "clumsiness."

The rain did not let up until we were almost within site of the tiny village of Hanamenu. It had been a difficult descent, and the four of us were extremely tired, since we had been in a great hurry to meet the *St. Maria* by mid-afternoon, as promised.

As we approached the village, we encountered a middle-aged man, clad only in dungarees, who carried a large sack of garden vegetables over his back. Although we had not met him earlier, he was obviously aware of us, and also about our plans to hike across the mountain that day. And, although none of us could speak French of Marquesean, and he did not know English, he made it very clear that he wanted to give us the sack of vegetables. It contained some very good looking lettuce, radishes, carrots, and tomatoes. After some hand signals, and once we understood his desire for us to take the vegetables, Mr. Camp offered him money in payment. But it immediately was obvious that our gardener was highly upset by the offer, and he became even more agitated when a second bill was produced. Although none of us knew what he said, we soon understood that his dignity had been damaged. He turned abruptly about and marched up the trail in the direction we had just come. We shouted our thanks as he stormed away, but did not have the time to follow him and beg forgiveness.

We continued down the path, though the tiny village to the beach, where we were picked up at the appointed time and place. The gift of the vegetables was greatly appreciated by the entire crew.

We never returned to Atuona, although we all wanted to visit that lovely place again. All of us for different reasons, I assume. I would have liked to spend another night with Katrina, but it was not to be. After a day exploring the northern slopes above Hanniapa, we set sail for the little island of Fatu Hiva, approximately 50 miles southeast of Hiva Oa. We had learned that the people living there had some sort of sickness, and our medical doctor wanted to see if he could help. We also had learned that the island had considerable undisturbed forest, running from the shoreline to the top of the rugged peaks. And so, that evening we anchored in Bon Repos Bay, on the southwestern corner of the island.

The village on Omoa was far more primitive than Atuona, and, in a sense, more compatible with what I had expected for the Marquesas. The village meeting place, where our doctor tended to the sick, was a grassy sward under a magnificent banyan tree. There is where the local people sat and visited all day long. And that is where we met Jacques, the Chief of Fatu Hiva. Unlike Hiva Oa, where the Governor managed the entire island, Fatu Hiva was run by a chief. It seemed to work very well, as we found an atmosphere of peace and tranquility.

That first evening we all sat under the banyan tree and got acquainted with the locals. The air was filled with heavy scents of flowers, but when the dancing begun, it was very different from the almost rowdy New Years party of Atuona. The dancers were extremely graceful, and their body motions and waving arms were a thing to behold. Chief Jacques explained that this was the native Polynesian dance.

Mr. Camp was extremely interested in the dance, and asked numerous questions about the meaning of the graceful gestures. Each movement had meaning. Mr. Camp was invited to participate, and we had a great laugh at his ungainly attempts to imitate the native dancers. But somehow, I found that his sincere efforts, as clumsy as they were, gave him a more down-to-earth personality. I liked him much more afterwards.

Our exploration of Fatu Hiva included a canoe trip up the bay and a short hike up the valley to a beautiful waterfall. The scenery was superb, and we all shed our clothes and bathed in the luscious, sweet waters. Ms. Clouster, fortunately, had remained aboard ship. All the while we were bathing, little fish nibbled at our bare skin. Mr. Graff was able to collect several, and the species was later identified as a fish completely new to science.

Also on Fatu Hiva, we took various forays along the shore with brief inland excursions. Although Ms. Clouster found a great number of new insects, which I packed out, the other scientists had only minimal success.

Our next stop was Vaitahu on Resolution Bay in the island of Tahuata, one of the smallest of the Marquesas Islands. After native Omoa, Vaitahu was totally unattractive. There were signs of European civilization everywhere. In fact, a French cargo ship was anchored in the bay, and its main cabin had been turned into a store. Numerous goods were sold to the natives that either swam or canoed out to buy. We also visited the store and found all sorts of clothing from woman's dresses to men's dungarees, colored cloth, belts, perfumes, gramophone records, mouth organs, cigarettes, patent medicines, and dozens of other items.

I found a beautiful wood carving of a tern that reminded me of the white terns we had collected on Hiva Oa. The price, however, was much more than I had available. But when I asked about the price, the man insisted on showing me several other pieces that were not on display. They were some of the most elegant wood carvings I had ever seen. Most were carved from very dark teak wood. Various birds, dolphins, whales, and sharks were represented in the collection. But none were as appealing to me as the very light colored tern that I could not afford. Oh how I wanted that piece. But I reminded myself that I was present only because of the agreement that I would receive only food and lodging.

Our principal reason for visiting Tahuata was to explore a nearby coral reef, one of the very few in the Marquesas. Arrangements were made for a guide and canoe, and the next day we spent a good part of the day paddling over the reef.

Having grown up in the Virgin Islands, where there are some marvelous coral reefs, I felt very much at home. No one else could dive and remain underwater for as long, and so I naturally became a valuable assistant to our marine biologist, Dr. Kagan. We collected a huge array of marine specimens that day, from colorful fishes to various crabs, octopuses, sea urchins, sponges, sea cucumbers, starfish, and a variety of sea shells.

One very curious thing occurred when I collected a very large conch. On handing it to Dr. Kagan, he discovered a number of tiny cardinal fish swimming about in the small cavity between the shell and the body. So, in collecting others, we discovered that each conch also contained young cardinal fish. Dr. Kagan decided that the conchs were providing a maternity habitat for these reef fish. He explained that the closely related cardinal fish is known to carry its eggs in its mouth until they hatch, and that the adult probably deposits the tiny fry into or nearby a conch for protection from their abundant predators. Conchs are grazers that feed on algae and other plant life that they find in the sand and fine gravels.

The conchs provided us with marvelous meals. We collected about two dozen of these large shells. By a single chop with a machete, one could severe the fleshy foot that could then be pulled free. These large muscles were delicious when sautéed in oil.

Because of our most welcome finds on the one coral reef, we decided to remain an additional day so that we could collect at a second reef a mile or two up the coast. I again accompanied Dr. Kagan, and we found three species of nudibranches, shell-fish without shells that are very slug-like in appearance.

All were of the genus *Doris*, according to Dr. Kagan, a pretty name for such an ugly creature. The largest of the three was dove-colored, dotted with brown spots, and yellowish gills and horns. The middle-sized nudibranch was a striking black color with large coral-pink patches all over its back and with a slaty-blue underside. But the third and smallest species was a true gem of the day's collection. It was a flat creamy white creature with rows of reddish purple spots and edged with brilliant orange.

The following day we sailed for Nuka Hiva, the largest and northern-most of the Marquesas Islands. This island was probably the best known of the islands because it was where author Herman Melville lived and wrote. We anchored in Taipi Bay during the late afternoon, with time for a short visit ashore. We immediately experienced the "nonos," a local, tiny, biting insect that we had been warned about. It actually is a sandfly that is so small that it usually is ignored until one feels its bite. In sucking blood, it will actually enlarge to a dull purplish color. And on brushing it away, a large spot of blood is left behind. The bites will often produce a slight fever.

Because of these irritating insects, the majority of the island's people lived at higher elevations, where the nonos were less numerous. Ms. Clouster, of course, was very interested in collecting a good sample of nonos, and so I was subjected to these ferocious creatures for several hours before we had an adequate sample. My arms and face were covered with welts.

My most enjoyable visit to Nuka Hiva was our day-long hike into Taipi Valley. Crossing a fruit plantation, Ms. Clouster, Mr. Johnson, Mr. Camp, and I entered the forest and followed a narrow path upward toward a mass of fallen rocks. In about a mile we reached a relatively open area with scattered trees and where the slopes were almost totally covered by enormous platforms of stones and rocks. Mr. Camp was elated. "This was once a great place of sacrifice for the inhabitants of Taipi," he explained. And he began to point out details of what had once been mighty monuments.

"The early South Seas islanders were very different than the fun-loving people we find today," he told us. "Some of the stones in this platform weigh many tons. Think what was involved with moving and positioning them without any sort of mechanical apparatus, just sheer muscular effort."

"But it would take hundreds of men. Where did they come from?" asked Ms. Clouster.

"There obviously was a much larger population then than there is today, and maybe in the entire Marquesas Islands," Mr. Camp responded. Then he added, "They undoubtedly had a very strong motive to build such great structures in this tropical climate. Religion was the driving force for erecting such structures."

"How were the structures utilized?" I asked.

Mr. Camp thought a few moments and then answered, "For rituals. Cannibalism probably was an important part of the ritual. Those early people had a very distorted view of religion." Then he pointed to some broken rocks and said, "There are some pieces of stone figures. The platform was probably adorned with hideous stone images. All part of the cannibalistic ceremonies."

"What could have initiated the early people to begin eating others?" I asked. "Was starvation, due to some major catastrophe, a reason?"

"Probably not," Camp answered. "Many early peoples believed that by eating their enemies they could somehow transfer their strength and bravery to themselves. That same concept was later adapted by the priests, who in time restricted the eating of human flesh to themselves as part of special ceremonies and to satisfy their gods."

All during the remainder of our stay on Nuka Hiva, the idea of ritualistic cannibalism was a point of discussion. The few natives that we met seemed to know little if anything about the earlier culture. Although they were aware of the ruins in the upper Taipi Valley, and they told Mr. Camp, who could speak some French, they knew nothing. They regarded them as little more than mysterious ruins from another world.

Chapter 6

It was a brilliant, sunny morning when we approached Tahiti. The island rose abruptly from the sea like a mighty fortress. Its great jagged peaks, green valleys, silvery cascades, and palm-fringed shores were all that I had dreamt it would be. It truly was an idyllic setting.

Towards noon we reached the mouth of Papeete Harbor, and it wasn't long before a local pilot in a small motorboat came out to guide us through the reef to the quiet lagoon. The pilot also brought us a mail sack, and everyone was soon engrossed in news from home. My mother's letter expressed hope that I would be coming home soon. She also informed me that her health had declined in recent weeks, but that she was receiving excellent care from Dr. Hormel, her long time doctor.

I, of course, was deeply concerned about my mother's health. But there was little that I could do, being so far away from home. So I immediately wrote a long, informative letter about my journey to date, wished her well, and posted it at the Papeete Post Office the next day.

Tahiti, the largest of the Society Islands, contains a varied environment. The island is divided into two sections, each an ancient volcanic cone, connected by a narrow corridor. Mt. Orohena, over 7,000 feet elevation, and with several smaller outlying peaks, dominates the larger, northern portion of the island. Mt. Rooniu, slightly more than 4,000 feet elevation, dominates the southern section. The northern coast is rugged and rocky, with few reefs, while the southern coast is broad and gentle with a rather extensive barrier reef.

But for all of Tahiti's raw beauty, I was most excited about its native wildlife and its women. During our entire voyage to date, our sailors had talked constantly about the beautiful women they expected to find there.

Most of the rumors were based on the tale of the mutinous crew of the *Bounty*. After getting rid of tyrannical Captain Blight, they had sailed back to Tahiti to claim their women before starting a new colony on Pitcairn Island. They had all risked their lives for their Tahitian sweethearts.

Now I was to see if the Tahitian women were as marvelous as the rumors suggested. And I was not disappointed in the least. The Tahitian women possessed a sultry beauty that is hard to resist. Dressed in their colorful but skimpy paheua, a brief cotton skirt with garlands of flowers, the very friendly native Tahiti's "vahines," as the young ladies were called, were the most tempting women I could imagine. Throughout our three-week stay on Tahiti, I must have fallen in love with a dozen or more vahines, each more appealing than the last. But I got involved with only one.

Tahiti also possessed dangers of a totally different kind. As strangers, we had no warning of the poisonous stonefish that resided around the island. Although there are no snakes on the islands, the blue waters of the quiet lagoons contain the sometimes lethal stonefish.

Henny got stung by one of these poisonous fish during the second afternoon, when he and several of the sailors were swimming. When climbing a rock that rose out of the water, he stepped on one of these well-camouflaged fish that was resting on the ledge. He immediately swam to the beach, and if one of the local medicine men had not treated him on the spot he might have died. As it was, Henny was bed-ridden and in considerable agony a good part of our stay in Tahiti.

Mr. Spenser later collected four of these foot-long, toxic fish. And on close examination, he found that each possessed a series of long spines along its back. Mr. Spenser explained, "A pair of poison sacs is located at the base of each spine. See here," as he pointed to the swollen sacs. "They are arranged so that any pressure extorted on the sacs ejects poisonous fluid along shallow grooves on either side of the spine, so that it can enter a wound caused by the sharp spine."

Henny's injury seemed to bring the villagers and our crew close together. Everyone, crew and villagers alike, came to his rescue. And afterward, I visited him almost daily in the village, where he was first treated and where he remained while recuperating.

It was during one of my first visits with Henny, while he was still in severe pain, that I met Rebecca. Her sister, Sarina, one of the town nurses, was caring for Henny, and so I naturally got acquainted with these two sisters. Although Sarina was totally dedicated to her patients, Rebecca was far more interested in the foreign visitors. And when she learned that I was an American, especially one her own age, she apparently decided that I was the man of her dreams.

Looking back at my relationship with Rebecca, I believe that I would have been far more interested in a long-term relationship if she had not been the aggressor. But in spite of spending many nights with her, and experiencing what she considered "truly love," I could never commit myself. And so I found myself seriously involved for short periods of time only, especially during the nights filled with passion.

But by morning I was anxious to explore the next valley or mountain slope. It was on our very first collecting trips on Tahiti that we found our first birdwing swallowtail. Ms. Clouster was already aware of these huge butterflies, but I was taken totally by surprise. "Ms. Clouster," I yelled, on seeing the first one, "look at that great black and blue butterfly. There on the passion flower. It must be a foot across."

"Oh, yes! That is a fine example of an Ornithoptera," she informed me. "Here, take the net and capture it."

It took several attempts before I proudly presented her with one of the giant butterflies. It measured 11 inches from wing tip to wing tip, and, up close it was a velvety black color, streaked with broad bands of iridescent green and blue. "You have captured a male," she said. "Females possess a velvety brown background, rather than black. We must find a female for the collection."

We found birdwing swallowtails reasonably common in moist openings in the forest throughout the middle elevations of the island. And before we departed, we had collected about two dozen specimens. Expect for their huge size and the amount of room each specimen took up in the collection, she would have collected hundreds. She explained how valuable the specimens might be for trading purposes for the museum.

Although I spent most of the days with Ms. Clouster, on the days she remained aboard ship, preparing specimens, I usually went with Mr. Johnson, helping him collect birds. Tahiti and all of the other Society Islands were a paradise for birds, seabirds as well as land birds. On one of those days, we rented a yacht and motored over to the smaller island of Moorea, off Tahiti's northwestern coastline. Moorea was a favorite site for seabirds, and Mr. Johnson wanted to collect a sample of what might be roosting there.

All went well in crossing the strait, negotiating the reef in a smaller boat, and reaching the island. The rocky cliffs were indeed covered with sea birds, and thousands soared overhead as we approached. Frigatebirds, boobies, gulls, and terns were there in abundance. Their guano not only smelled to high heaven, but it made the rocky slopes and high ledges extremely slick. Each excursion on the cliffs to recover shot birds was extremely dangerous. By the end of the day, I was covered with the smelly, sticky, white goo.

When it was finally time to leave Moorea for our return to Papeete, my associates would not allow me into the boat until I had taken a long, cleansing bath, clothes and all, in the surf. And when we started back to the yacht, we discovered that the tide was out and we could not ride over the reef. After an hour of trying to find a better route, we retreated to a little beach to lighten the load before trying to ferry just two passengers at a time. We soon discovered that any more than a single person was too much weight. So, we sent one of the sailors back to the yacht to tell the owner, who had remained on board, about our predicament, and that we would have to wait until high tide.

We all sat on the beach with our great load of specimens, awaiting the change in tide. In about an hour we began to detect a rise. But then we began to realize that we were situated on a narrow beach, at the foot of the slippery cliff that was gradually disappearing with the rising tide. We also understood that if we were caught by the tide, we might be swept out onto the reef. We would not only loose all our specimens but, possibly, our lives as well. Our boat had not yet returned. Not knowing about our predicament, they had decided to wait until the tide was adequate to transport us all at the same time. It was a very serious predicament.

"Hi, yo," someone yelled from around the cliff face. "Hi, yo," we all yelled back in unison. And suddenly, a canoe, with a lone old man at the helm, came into view, and glided over the reef to what little beach remained. I was never so glad to see anyone as much as that old man and his canoe. It was a great, broad canoe, that I could not help but wonder how it could be handled by a lone boatman.

The old man could speak little more English than "hi," but he understood the danger we were in. We immediately loaded ourselves and specimens into the ancient canoe, finishing just as the last of our beach became covered with the rising tide. The canoe sat high in the water, even loaded with eight men and 800 pounds or more of specimens. We never did understand where the old man had come from or where he was going. No one could speak to him, although among us we could speak several languages. But we all were most thankful for his timely appearance. In less than an hour we had crossed the reef and reached the yacht, a distance about a quarter-mile.

He left us off at the yacht, and before we could thank him properly with some token of our appreciation, he continued on his way with barely a wave. We had learned an important lesson that day. But we never did see our mysterious rescuer again.

The next two days it rained so hard that we all stayed on board, preparing specimens in one of the cabins and catching-up on our notes. The lull in our collecting activities also allowed for letter-writing and games. I wrote another long letter to my mother and stepfather describing Tahiti in considerable detail.

I also attempted to describe the changes that had occurred in the Tahitian peoples since the island was first found by Captain Cook. Mr. Jensen had told us that Captain Cook had estimated the population in 1779 at about 150,000, but that number had declined to 15,000 in 1810, and an 1815 census recorded only 8,000 souls. The native Polynesians had no defense against the diseases, including tuberculosis, smallpox, measles and whooping cough that the European sailors had brought with them.

Chess was the game of choice for both the scientists and the crew. Mr. Ashley considered himself a real chess expert, and he soon challenged everyone aboard. No one could match his skill, and so he beat all challengers. However, several days later at sea, one of the sailors, who had not played during the two rainy days, beat him two out of three games. Mr. Ashley was obviously shaken, and refrained from any additional challenges.

The rain stopped rather suddenly late in the afternoon of the second day, and sunset that evening was truly spectacular.

Later, all the scientists went ashore to attend the "Governor's Ball." It was a fancy affair, held in a large, grand hall. More than 100 couples attended, and we danced until dawn to an excellent jazz band.

I did little dancing, but I thoroughly enjoyed the band. They played old standards that I had grown-up to. The combination of good music, considerable drink, and the colorful dress worn by all the local dancers, provided me with a night I will long remember.

Tahiti's upland forest was some of the most beautiful I had ever seen. But it was an extremely wet environment, with numerous streams flowing down the steep slopes. Every little valley had one or a series of waterfalls, many of them starting high above the valley floor. The interior of the island was accessible only by steep and rugged footpaths. I was sure that many of them had never before been seen by Americans or Europeans. Each trip into the hinterlands was, for me, a great adventure. Even today, when I think of the South Seas, I do not think of the numerous beaches and marvelous bays and coves, or even the friendly women, but of the sparkling waterfalls among Tahiti's tropical greenery.

I made several trips into those marvelous forests during our stay. Mr. Johnson managed to collect specimens of all his target birds. One species, a large and shiny, blue-green fruit pigeon, that he claimed was endemic only to Tahiti and Makatea Islands, was fairly common in the forest. And we discovered that it was a favorite food of the natives, who shot them whenever possible. And as soon as they learned that it was one of our target birds, we received more than two dozen as gifts. If he had not told them that we did not have further room, I am sure that they would have wiped out the last remaining individual. As it was, I couldn't help but wonder how long these unique pigeons could stand the steady hunting.

And the impact of such actions and others became the topic of discussion that night at supper. Both Mr. Johnson and Mr. Cutter were most knowledgeable about such issues. "Some of the gravest damage to native flora and fauna has resulted from the extensive conversion of native forests to agriculture," Johnson said. "Sugar cane and coffee have replaced some of the island's most outstanding forests," he added. "And large tracts of land have also been cleared for grazing lands for cattle and sheep."

Mr. Cutter stated that, "Native island species have also been depleted by a variety of introduced species. Pigs that were brought to the islands as a food source and European rats, that have been transported by sailing ships and either climbed down the ropes or swam to shore, have literally changed the native scene over the years."

"Yes," said Johnson, "rats and pigs especially have had disastrous effects on seabird colonies."

"Don't forget the mongoose that is now being introduced on all the sugar cane islands to prey on the rats," Cutter said. He added: "European rats became so abundant in canefields that when the cane was cut the rats literally overran the island, entering homes and eating whatever they could find. The local people became understandably upset. So then the governments introduced the mongoose to eat the rats, without once thinking about the consequences."

Mr. Cutter shook his head, and then continued: "They apparently never asked a biologist about this project. Rats are active mostly at night and can build nests in a wide variety of sites, from among vegetation on the ground to shrubs and taller trees. The mongoose is a diurnal mammal that will eat practically any living creatures that it comes in contact with. But they don't climb trees. So all the intended victims had to do was to spend more time in trees and they totally eliminated chance encounters with mongooses."

"But," said Johnson, "they then found other easy prey of ground-nesting birds and other creatures, including many of them unique to only a single island that was active during the daytime."

Not long before we were to leave Tahiti, I accompanied Mr. Ashley, Dr. Kagan and Mr. Johnson on an overnight yacht trip to the far side of the island. We arrived at the village of Mataiea during the late afternoon, and went ashore to find a guide and to rent horses for a six-mile trip into the interior to Lake Vaihiria the following day. Ashley had learned about a floppy-eared eel, locally known as "puhi taria," that lived in the lake's cold water, and he intended to collect samples.

The following morning, we followed a trail along the Vaihiria River, crossing it more than 20 times between the beach and spectacular Vaihiria Lake. It shined like a blue jewel in a bright green setting. Although the morning was bright and sunny, clouds moved into the valley by mid-day, and torrents of rain fell on us all afternoon until we returned to the yacht.

We managed to capture only one eel, and we probably would not have managed that if it had not been for our guide. He knew where to look, and how to hook this elongated fish with only minimal effort. However, taking the squirming, slippery, six-foot eel out of the water and confining it in a large gunny sack that we had brought along for that purpose, was something else again. The eel was extremely strong, and it took three of us to control the thrashing creature before Mr. Spenser could inject it with chloroform to subdue it. That effort took us almost an hour, and I was glad that our catch was limited to one. By the time we started back down the trail, we were all soaked to the skin.

The day before our departure, I accompanied Captain Bonney and his assistant to Papeete to purchase supplies. Our food had run extremely low, and this was to be our last major port before again striking out across the Pacific.

Most of the stores we visited were operated by Europeans, but the Papeete market, where we did most of our shopping, was operated by Tahitians. It contains every fruit and vegetable possible. There were huge piles of melons, mangoes, bananas, oranges, limes, guavas, passion fruit, and avocados. Vegetables were almost as numerous. Potatoes were the one exception; they had to be imported and were very expensive.

Meats and fish were abundant, as well. Pork was a staple, but chicken, ducks, and even turkey were also plentiful. And the fish market was stacked with freshly caught fish of every color and shape imaginable.

Except for fish, that we readily caught at sea, we purchased more than I thought we could possible use. It required an ancient truck to transport it all back to the dock.

On our last evening at Tahiti, the islanders invited the entire crew to a party on the beach. And what a party it was. Plenty of food and drink, and the villagers treated us to some amazing Polynesian dances.

Rebecca knew by then that I would be leaving her soon, and she was obviously sad throughout the evening. She sat so close that I could hardly move, and she whispered her love to me all during the dances. Finally, sometime after midnight, the partiers begin to disperse, two at a time. And I soon followed Rebecca to her thatch-covered shack for the very last time.

I slept very little that night, as I too was sorry that I would be leaving Rebecca behind. She never suggested that she might go with me, but several times she asked when I would be returning for her. She took much for granted.

Our love-making was a sad-sweet affair. But at dawn I left her sleeping and rowed out to the *St. Maria*. By mid-morning, we lifted anchor and motored out of the bay.

Although dozens of Tahitian friends lined the shore to bid us farewell, Rebecca was nowhere in sight.

It took us almost 24 hours to reach the Austral Islands that form the southern end of French Polynesia. We continued southeast throughout the day, passing the islands of Rurutu, Tubai, and Raivavae, across the Tropic of Capricorn, before approaching Rapa, our destination. We were further south than we had been at any time on our voyage, and a drop in temperature was obvious. The seas had been high for a couple days, and we had a difficult time approaching Rapa against a stiff gale. In fact, the wind was so strong that we were forced to tack as best we could for almost two days.

Finally, on our fourth day out, still with strong, gusty winds, we decided to head for the protection of Ahurei Bay, a great indentation on Rapa's east side. Although the entrance was guarded by several large reefs, the French Government had set up red and black beacons to guide a ship through the reefs. And as we very slowly steamed into the bay, a whaleboat approached with a pilot, who was soon aboard.

However, driven by the winds, we had drifted too far to the right, and try as we might, we were unable to adjust our direction in time. We suddenly felt our bottom crunch into a reef, and in another instant we were aground.

Captain Bonney immediately ordered the two lifeboats lowered over the side. We knew that we were fast on the reef, and if the sharp coral was sticking through the ship's bottom, we could sink in no time. The ship could then easily slip past the reef into several hundred feet of water. In less than an hour's time, the scientists and their belongs were in the lifeboats, and we started toward the shore.

Henny told me later about what happened. "Captain Bonney tried every way to free us," he said. "Full speed ahead, then full speed astern, but no way. Every few minutes I felt a grinding noise as thee ship bumped the coral. I could see only clouds of milky water and broken pieces. I tell you, Greg, I never thought we wood escape."

"The mates in thee engine-room could barely keep their feet. Edwards yelled that we were fast by the stern, that thee rudder post was being forced up. Suddenly, a great gust of wind hit us, and the entire ship shuttered. I thought we're lost. Then Edwards screamed, 'By God, she's off!' And she was."

"A second later," Henny added, "the engines were put full forward, and with thee force of a tail wind, we pulled forward into thee channel. My God, whod a relief."

It took another couple hours for the pilot to guide the ship through the maze of reefs into the inner harbor. The lifeboats had gone on to the beach, and by evening we all were back on board. We returned to the ship with much appreciation for the ship and crew.

By morning the dark clouds and wind of the previous days had disappeared, and the best of Rapa lay before us. We were anchored in about the middle of the bay, completely sheltered from the sea outside. The shore was extensive and the hills behind were little more than nipples, compared with the ragged peaks of Tahiti. The highest peak of Mount Perahu was about 2,000 feet elevation. The village of Ahurei consisted of only a few dozen thatched huts, partially hidden among a mass of dark green orange and coffee trees, and a single white church, its high steeple rising above all the rest of the town.

The scientists landed on the beach, amid a bevy of youngsters, each seemingly happier than the next. They all shouted, laughed, and grinned at us as we made our way up the single roadway to the valley beyond. We all experienced a full but uneventful day, returning to the ship at dusk. It was then that we received the good news that a diver, who had examined our hull, had reported only minor damage from the incident with the reef. Some of the copper plates had been torn away and the teak planking had been scratched and splintered, but it all could be repaired in an estimated four days. We could then continue our voyage to Easter Island and back to Panama.

The next morning on landing, we were greeted by three young women, each with colorful pareus and huge, lovely smiles. We soon discovered that Jennei, a lovely creature of about 20 years of age, spoke some English, and was there to offer her services as interpreter and guide during our stay.

"How do you know English?" Mr. Johnson asked. "I marry English sailor, who now gone home," she answered. And she slowly relayed her story about how an English ship had been lost on the Nelson Reef, about 120 miles to the northeast, and the crew, taking to their boats, had reached this island. They remained on Rapa for almost a year before a trading schooner arrived and took them to Tahiti. The sailors had all taken wives, and Hanamai and a few others had learned a little English.

"Do you know husband?" she asked. She had no idea why our British sailors did not know her husband.

Nevertheless, Jennei was very helpful during our short stay. And we even met her parents and a son, Johnny, named after his British father. We saw several other partially white children, all about the same age, during our stay. The shipwrecked sailors had certainly left their mark behind when they returned to their own world.

I wondered how many more partially white children would result from the voyage of the *St. Maria*.

Chapter 7

Easter Island was without doubt the most remote place on earth. And also one of most depauperate. It is the southernmost of the Polynesian islands, but too cold for coconut palms and coral reefs.

It took us almost three weeks of sailing practically due east from Rapa before we spied the sprawling landscape of Easter Island. And since the island possessed but two bays with sandy beaches, we stayed off-shore until the next morning. We finally dropped anchor in Anakena Bay, along the northern shore, in mid-morning. It was here at Anakena Bay in the twelfth century where the first Easter Island King, Hotu Matua, arrived by canoe, according to legend.

From all appearances, the island was completely devoid of human civilization. Although we could see a few sheep and cattle grazing at the far distance on the open grasslands, no other living creatures were evident.

We knew that the village of Hanga Roa was situated across the island along the western shore, and we understood that we were obligated to contact island officials upon our arrival. We also needed to obtain assistance during our visit. So a small group was selected to hike the approximately ten miles across the island to the village to make contact with the appropriate individuals.

Although I was eager to join the hikers, Ms. Clouster had other ideas. She wanted to do some collecting early-on. Since she had finished preparing all the insect specimens we had so far collected, she wanted to investigate the grasslands to see what insects might be present. She was well aware of the extensive abuse Easter Island had experienced over the centuries, and she was curious about what hardy species might still exist.

Easter Island has had a long history of human use, although a good part of its historic past is based on speculation. Mr. Camp, our archeologist, was most knowledgeable about Easter Island. His desire to visit the island, in fact, was the principal reason that we had come so far east. During a conversation a few days earlier, Camp had told us about the real significance of the island.

"Easter Island is the site of a forgotten civilization," he said. "The original inhabitants, known as Rapanui, probably Polynesians, were an extraordinary society. They possessed the only written language in Polynesia, although it is still undeciphered. The Rapanui also quarried the island's rocky hills to build innumerable large, stone figures, called 'moai.' How the massive, slender figures were somehow moved from the quarry to various parts of the island and placed on rock platforms, and how the huge rock turbans or hats were placed on top of most of the figures, is anyone's guess. And how the moai were moved from their quarry to the final position on the island is a true mystery." With that, he paused, I suppose to let us wonder about the importance of his dialog.

Camp continued. "Dutch explorer and Admiral Jacob Roggeveen, who discovered the island on Easter Sunday, 1722 - hence the name - found that the residents he encountered knew nothing about the stone figures. They claimed that the treeless island was good for little more than raising cattle and sheep."

"How large are the stone figures?" someone had asked.

Camp responded that they varied in size, "some as much as eight meters, and estimated at 20 or more tons."

Most of us were fascinated about how the great figures could have been moved, and also how they might be righted once on-site. And how could a stone hat be placed on top of each?

Mr. Nichols, our botanist, provided us with one method of possible transportation. "The complete removal of the islands trees suggest that the trees were utilized to slide the figures about," he said. "The trees could also be used for constructing towers for righting the figures and installing their top hats," he added.

Nichols then speculated about how the complete removal of the island's entire forest might affect the island. "Once the tree cover was lost, a windy island such as Easter would quickly loose much of its top soils. With the lose of the top soils, the terrain could no longer support woody vegetation. It would be only a matter of time before any viable human civilization would begin its inevitable decline."

"How long ago did all this happen?" I asked.

"No one knows for sure, the statues were constructed between 500 and 1600," Mr. Camp answered. "However," he continued, "by the time Chile annexed the island in 1888, the landscape was of little use except for grazing stock."

"Sheep was the principal stock," Nichols added. "Sheep more than likely eliminated what little woody vegetation still existed."

Over the next several days, throughout our stay at Easter Island, I replayed that conversation in my mind time and again. It became abundantly clear to me that man can easily destroy his environment, and eventually himself, as well, by ignoring some of the basic principles of land management. The ancient Rapanui had been wise enough to develop their own written language, but so foolish that they destroyed their own culture because they did not respect their natural environment. The only truly healthy environment is one that contains numerous habitats, so that if one part fails, for whatever reason, others will continue to support its inhabitants.

It was an important lesson, and I talked with various scientists about this issue throughout the remainder of the voyage.

Shortly after dropping anchor in Anakena Bay, we boarded the boat that was to take the hikers to shore. After landing, I watched them stride off across the gentle but rocky terrain. I remained to assist Ms. Clouster.

She decided that we would collect along a great loop route so that we would be back at the beach to meet the boat by late afternoon. I was loaded down, as usual, with a huge backpack filled with collecting jars and our lunches.

Almost immediately we discovered one of the stone figures, lying facedown besides a scattering of rocks that had once been a large platform. Nearby was what appeared to be a great reddish rock hat that undoubtedly had once sat atop its head. On closer examination of the weathered, lava figure, we could make out the outlines of its arms and hands. The fingers were very long and all the same length; it appeared that the hands were clasping the sides of its abdomen. I estimated that the figure measured about 20 feet in length.

Insects were few and far between along our route; at least in comparison with collections at most of the other sites we had visited on our voyage. Grasshoppers, crickets, and beetles dominated the collection, and included a carrion beetle that Ms. Clouster got very excited about. She had not seen it before, and thought that it might have been new for science.

All during our day-long hike across the landscape, I watched for signs of other wildlife. Except for an occasional frigatebird, a pelagic species, that soared high overhead, and a few larks that flew off on our approach, no other animals were seen.

We did find numerous other stone figures, all fallen over and in the same sorry state of disrepair. And, in searching for insects along the base of a volcanic outcrop, I discovered a number of petroglyphs. These crude carvings were barely discernible, they were so badly weathered. But on careful examination I was able to identify a human-like creature with broad shoulders and a strange bird-head.

Late afternoon found us back on board the *St. Maria*, where several of the sailors had spent a successful day fishing. They had caught four very odd-looking groupers, with huge red eyes, along the rocky shore. Our evening meal was wonderful.

The hiking party did not return until the middle of the next day. They arrived in a horse-drawn buggy, along with several officials on horseback. The owner of the buggy was a Mr. Collins, a Scotsman who leased the majority of the island from the Chilean Government. He had agreed to take us to Hano Aroi Crater, in the center of the island, as well as to Orongo to the south. Arrangements also had been made for a boat to meet us at Orongo in two days that would take us out to the sea-stacks off the South Cape, a nesting and roosting site for sea-birds.

After dinner that evening, Mr. Collins answered numerous questions about himself and Easter Island. He seemed genuinely pleased to be with strangers. It had been more than a year, he told us, since he had last visited with anyone from the British Isles. He was eager to hear news of home. But we had been away for so many months that we had little to tell him that he did not already know about.

Although he had been raised in Scotland, he had gone off to see the world more than 30 years earlier, and he had returned to Scotland only once since. He had raised cattle in both Venezuela and southern Argentina for several years, and had moved to Easter Island almost 18 years earlier. He intended to improve the breed of sheep being raised there. But, he told us, although he had tried a variety of methods to increase the viability and nutrients of the grasses, by burning and rotating grazing patterns, he had little success to date. He admitted that he was experiencing a very marginal business. "But," he said in a Scottish accent, "I've fallen in love with Easter Isle. Aye, I have no intention to leave, ever."

The course of the conversation eventually got back to the one great hallmark of Easter Island, the abundant stone figures and how they were transported from the quarry to their final destinations. Collins's theory was that they had been placed on great wooden sleds and dragged to where they were intended.

"Where had the timbers come from to build the sleds?" Mr. Nichols asked.

"There once was a rather significant forest with huge native palms and hardwoods in the lowlands and a toromiro forest on the slopes of Rana Raraku," he answered. "There is still small stands of toromiro shrubs up there. You will see for yourselves, tomorrow."

After a brief pause, he continued, "Me own theory 'bout the island's history is that it was covered with forest when it was first settled, probably a thousand years ago. Those first peoples possessed a sophisticated culture, complete with skills in organization and engineering. But they did not understand how to manage land. With the increase of population and subsequent increased use of the island's natural resources, the island's forests were eventually removed. By the time Captain Cook visited the island in 1775, he found only 630 inhabitants, barely surviving in a barren environment. A far cry from the estimated 12,000 inhabitants that once occurred here at the cultural apex in the sixteenth century."

Collins paused briefly, and then continued, "Like cattle, once a population exceeds its capacity to live off the land, nothing can be done until that population declines to a point where it can again be sustained by adequate resources."

"It is like the Irish potato," Mr. Nichols added. "All of Ireland was dependent upon that single crop. Until 1845, that is, when the potato crop was infected by a parasitic fungus that killed the plants. Ireland was devastated. More than half the population died or emigrated elsewhere. All because of their dependency on a single crop."

Someone asked about the meaning of the stone figures, and that question solicited a long discourse on various theories. But each were of religious connotation. "The bottom line," Collins explained, "was that the moai served as gods. They were placed all around the island, all facing inward, as well as at various inland sites, where they were intended to guard the inhabitants against evil spirits and outside invaders."

After some additional questions and answers about the figures, Collins brought up a completely new topic. "Do you know 'bout the rongo-rongo tablets?"

Mr. Camp was first to respond. "Yes, indeed, I have seen one of the tablets at the Royal Museum."

"Aye," answered Collins. "They are pieces of driftwood with several lines of writing. Every other line is upside down. I am told that they represent the only known writing in all of ancient Polynesia."

"Several scholars of ancient languages have examined the tablets, but none have been able to decipher their meaning," Mr. Camp added.

I was still curious about the statues, but hesitant to change the topic again. But after several minutes, when the discussion about the tablets seemed to be getting nowhere, I boldly asked, "Excuse me, but why aren't any of the moai still standing erect? What happened to them?"

"Ah yes," Collins responded, "I'm told that a second wave of Polynesians, probably from the Marquesas, arrived and massacred the original people in 1670. The new inhabitants maintained the moia, but experienced a period of cultural decline, including much internecine fighting, that lasted until the mid-1800s. All of the moai were felled by the time Captain Cook visited the island in 1774."

Collins added, "These later people, the ancestors of the few current, native inhabitants, practiced cannibalism."

It was late in the night before any of us retired to our beds. And I spend another hour or more rehashing the fascinating discussion in which I had participated. I was especially intrigued that all the great statues had been placed facing inland, rather than facing seaward. I would think that the early peoples would have faced them outward as a warning to possible invaders. But facing them all inward suggested perhaps that they were overly obsessed with themselves and totally unaware of any other peoples.

The next day, we did not go ashore and get underway until mid-morning. Ms. Clouster and Mr. Collins rode in the buggy, which also carried our supplies for the three-day excursion. Messieurs Johnson, Camp, Ashley, and Professor Carnell and I walked, although Johnson took occasional rest periods by riding one of the horses for short distances.

By noon we had reached the rim of Rana Aroi, the highest point on the island. The views from the top were spectacular in all directions. The gradual slopes of the crater contained dozens of fallen moai among the lush grasslands. In the distance, the Atlantic Ocean looked very placid, and the two little islands of Motu Nui and Motu were evident just off the southern tip of the island.

Mr. Nichols examined the stunted toromiro shrubs along the crater rim. These relicts were all bent and twisted from the constant wind. But even these showed evidence of cutting. When asked about what possible use these little plants might be to the local inhabitants, Mr. Collins explained that their extremely hard wood was in much demand for carving. "Several of the native carvers make beautiful figures that they sell to visiting sailors. It is one of the very few island industries."

But it was the crater floor, directly below us a few hundred feet that commanded our attention. It contained a surprising large lake, partially filled with reeds and other water-loving plants. It was one of the few places I had so far seen on Easter Island that appeared to possess a natural habitat.

Mr. Nichols was first to express what we all were thinking. "We must explore the lake in the crater. It is sure to possess a variety of native plants and animals. The habitat may be a last stronghold of Easter Island relicts."

But what a disappointment it turned out to be. In spite of searching the shoreline and even wading into the reeds, the only animals species detected were insects. Ms. Clouster and I collected several hundred specimens, including a variety of odd-looking flies.

By the time we had finished our exploration of the wetland, it was too late to continue. So, we decided to camp along the grassy shore. And by the time we continued on to the south the next morning, we were several hours behind our intended schedule. Mr. Collins sent one of the horsemen ahead to Orongo to tell our boatman about our late arrival.

It wasn't until mid-afternoon before we arrived at Orongo, too late in the day for a safe visit to the off-shore sea-stacks. The ocean was extremely rough, and it was obvious that we would need to wait until morning.

We spent the remainder of the day exploring the steep, rocky shoreline about Orongo. Dr. Kagan and Mr. Spenser collected a large number of marine invertebrates, including a number of specimens that they claimed represented significant range extensions. They were species that had never before been collected so far east in the Atlantic.

Mr. Johnson and I wandered to the southern tip of the island, so that we could better see the birdlife soaring about the off-shore sea-stacks. We identified frigatebirds, gulls, numerous sooty terns, a few masked boobies, and a lone red-tailed tropicbird. Further out to sea, Johnson discovered a petrel that he thought was a Kermadec petrel. None came close enough to attempt a shot, however.

We also found a number of stone houses, with very low, narrow doorways, on the grassy headlands. Each was surrounded by rocks containing petroglyphs, far more intricately designed than those Ms. Clouster and I had found two days before. None of us were small enough to enter the shelters, and I could hardly wait for the opportunity to ask Mr. Collin about those odd structures.

As expected, Mr. Collins had a fascinating explanation for the rock structures. "They are remnants of the birdman cult that once existed on the island," he told us. "Once each year, when the seabirds return to nest, many of the islanders would gather at Orongo to squeeze themselves into the stone shelters to pray to their gods and hold special rites. Their annual vigil came to a climax when they risked their lives swimming to Moto Nui and Moto Lei to obtain an egg of the sooty tern. The first individual to successfully return with an egg was declared birdman of the year, a great honor among the birdman cult."

"That is truly amazing," Mr. Johnson said. "That is an extremely dangerous act. Was their much loss of life?" he asked.

"Indeed there was," Collin answered. "It was their method of obtaining recognition among their clan. And I'm told that is was an event the members prepared for all the rest of the year."

The island officials cooked up a wonderful breakfast the next morning, complete with coffee, eggs, cheese, and bread. Mr. Johnson complimented the cooks, and asked them where they had obtained the eggs. The answer stunned most of us.

"Yesterday morning, the boat crew landed on the island and collected the eggs, fresh off the nests," replied Mr. Collins. "You are eating tern eggs," he added. And he showed us an additional 30 or 40 eggs, carefully wrapped in cloth that would be taken back to Hanga Roa after our visit to the sea-stacks.

It was all we could do to refrain from chastising Mr. Collins and the boat crew for robbing the nests. But they were our hosts, and it was not the time nor place to preach about protecting seabird nesting sites.

But the morning boat trip to the two tiny islands was not as productive as we had hoped it would be. On approaching the island, the entire mass of birds departed and, except for one sooty tern that got close enough to shoot, they all stayed at a considerable distance. They apparently were spooked from the previous day's activities.

The lone sooty tern fell into the foamy waters at the edge of Mota Rei after it was shot, and Mr. Johnson had a very difficult time retrieving it. The sea was rougher than expected, and it was impossible to get close enough to the rocky face of the island. The specimen was finally retrieved by throwing a life ring out numerous times before it fell over the tern. Then he was able to pull it closer to where it could be picked up from the bow of the boat. Everyone on the boat came back to shore thoroughly soaked.

The long ride back to Anakena Bay and the *St. Maria* was with heavy heart. For the scientists, the three-day trip had been close to a disaster. We had struck out in the crater as well as at the South Cape sea-stacks. On the other hand, Mr. Camp had seen hundreds of moai. And, while the rest of us had remained at Orongo to attempt to collect some seabirds, he and Mr. Ashley had visited the rock shelters on the South Cape highland.

As might be expected at this point in a voyage, with no additional sites to visit, everyone was eager to head for home. So, after a farewell dinner aboard the *St. Maria*, we said farewell to Mr. Collins and the remaining officials, who headed for home. And by mid-morning the next day, we lifted anchor and began our long trip toward the northwest and Panama.

Chapter 8

Panama was still a long sail to the northwest, more than four weeks away. We made about 100 miles each day with decent wind. The first half of the trip went very well, with fair breezes and plenty of work to fill the time. The weather was exceptionally dry, however, which meant that our water supply went faster than we planned. So, by the third week out, we were forced to short rations and no bathing. But none of us seemed to mind. We were making good progress and we all had great expectations for our return to Panama. I even dreamt about finding another Suzana. I also intended to find Beaman and maybe help with some additional collecting. And I also looked forward to whatever mail might be waiting for me.

Early in our fourth week after leaving Easter Island, somewhere north of the Equator and after passing Cocos Island, only about one week out of Balboa, we encountered a fierce gale with heavy rain. We later discovered that it was a forecast of more to come.

At first the rain seemed like a Godsend, as we all hurried on deck to gather fresh water in whatever containers we could find. Even in that driving rainstorm, we welcomed the change in weather and the opportunity that the fresh water would provide for showers and clean clothing. That storm lasted for most of the day, but abated at dusk, and we experienced a truly quiet night, making less than one-third of our normal progress.

But dawn arrived with more evidence of stormy weather. A tall bank of dark clouds clung to the horizon directly in our path. We could see distant lightning. It was an ominous sight, but our current position seemed safe enough to continue under full sail. It was obvious, however, that the captain and crew were nervous. Captain Bonney checked the barometer on several occasions.

For awhile it appeared that we were actually following the clouds, that we would not be affected. But suddenly, at mid-morning, a strong and gusty wind came up so fast that it surprised us all. The dark clouds that had been ahead of us seemed to turn around and surround us. In no less than an hour the *St. Maria* was engulfed in the strongest, most active storm, with torrents of rain that we had experienced at anytime during our journey.

Captain Bonney immediately barked out orders: "All hands on deck! Lower away the upper topsail and haul up the foresail!" All of the ship's crew seemed to react at once, each with his own responsibility. I wondered at the time when they had been so well trained. Henny later told me that they all had early-on been given responsibilities for just such an emergency, before I had joined the crew. But there were times during the next several hours that I questioned my sanity for being there at all.

The storm was so heavy that it totally blotted out the sun. The day was almost as dark as night, except when the brilliant flashes of lightning illuminated the wild scene. The sea on all sides seemed to engulf our vessel, and the deck was totally awash with foamy water that rolled this way and that like a great mixer. Except for a few of the sailors who had already been on duty when the storm hit, and had already been clad in oilskins, the rest of us became completely soaked in no time at all.

I made my way forward to where the second officer was shouting orders to a crew, who were attempting to pull the ropes that controlled the foresail. While six men were all that were normally required, almost twice that number could barely make any progress at all against the great gusts of wind and rain that tore at the sail. "More beef," he yelled. And so I waded through the foam toward the nearest rope, where I joined in the strenuous tugging efforts. We all pulled with all our might. It took us more than an hour of very slow progress before we had the sail secured. There were times when we seemed to be loosing ground, and I expected the foresail to tear apart at any moment.

In the meantime, Captain Bonney had gone to the bridge to assist the man at the wheel in keeping the ship dead before the wind, an essential maneuver if the ship was going to stay upright through the storm. The hurricane-like conditions could easily sink a ship, even one as sea-worthy as the *St. Maria*, without the proper heading.

I later estimated the waves as high as eighty feet, one after the other. One could look up and see those mighty waves about to swallow the ship. I wondered how we could possibly escape being totally inundated. But somehow the *St. Maria* climbed those waves, time and time again. At the very top it was like looking into a deep valley, and we would start down, only to go right back up onto the next crest. We rode through that storm for what seemed like hours and hours. It was a truly wondrous ship, and with a marvelous crew!

I barely had time to finish my first task of assisting with the foresail before I was told to help tie down any of the loose objects that might still be on deck. So I dashed about attempting to find and secure what little remained. Except for two wooden buckets that seemed to be floating about, little else was found. These I emptied and took below where I found a scene of utter desolation. Water had blown in from various openings, and the floor was awash. Although the various odds-and-ends were safe from washing overboard, they were sloshing about as if they were on deck instead.

The storm was continuing to roar unabated when I return to the deck, but from the appearance of the sailors it was obvious that everything had been done that could possibly be done. Now, it was just a matter of keeping the ship into the wind and waiting out the storm. For another hour the wind blew as hard as ever, and the rain continued to fall in sheets; visibility was less than the length of the ship. Then the gusts became less often and less violent, and the torrents of rain became more normal, with smaller waves that did not wash over the deck. And two hours later the sky began to brighten and the sea seemed to be back almost to normal. Shortly afterward, when the sun set in the west, I witnesses the most incredible sunset ever. The magentas, red, and pinks, that streaked the entire western sky, were truly out of this world! Behind us, the black sky of the storm was streaked with lightning.

The next two days seemed almost normal, except for the rather extensive work of cleaning up both the deck and cabins. Remarkably we had suffered only minor damage, and that was easily repaired. And we had lost only a few nonessentials. I expect that much of the success in managing the storm was due to the fast-thinking of the knowledgeable crew.

I later heard Captain Bonney state that the storm was "one of the most violent and sudden" he had experienced in his 20-odd years of sailoring. And Henny told me that only once before, during a crossing between The Azores and the West Indies, had he experienced a worse storm.

So we all were more than anxious to reach Panama. But once again the sea had other plans for us. The fourth day after the storm was perfectly calm, without a whisper of a breeze. The sea looked like a plate of glass. And yet we were only two normal sailing days out of port. But we made little more than eight to ten miles a day. On the third day of calm, late in the evening we sighted land, and we all cried out in anticipation of reaching port and whatever else we were awaiting. But when we awoke the following morning the land had disappeared. We had drifted east. The mood of the crew, all of us for that matter, went from jubilation of the evening before, when we had seen land, to as low as it had been at any time during our journey.

By the end of that day, the sixth day of calm, the Captain informed us at supper that, "If tomorrow remains the same, we will burn what little coal we have left, and attempt to make port." He estimated that we had only about eight hours of coal remaining.

The morning conditions had not changed, so the engines were started and we began a faster but costly progress toward the west and Panama. By mid-day it was obvious that we did not have sufficient coal reserve to make it all the way. The sailors were obviously concerned. Henny said that it was entirely possible to drift eastward again. Then the word came that Captain Bonney had sent a wireless message to Balboa, asking for a tug to come out and tow us in. He had received an immediate response that a tug would get underway soon and meet as the following morning. The mood on deck changed again to happy anticipation.

A large tugboat arrived the next morning. We then made slow but steady progress toward port. By mid-afternoon, we were docked and giving thanks that we had all arrived safely. It was the first solid land we had seen after our recent experiences at sea. It was most welcome.

But then came time to say farewell to my shipmates. And it was not an easy task. We all shook hands, and both Mr. Johnson and Mr. Graff told me that if I was ever in need of work, they would be glad to find me a place. Ms. Clouster said little more than a casual goodbye. Afterwards, Henny and I spend the first part of the evening on shore, toasting one another and our various experiences. Then Henny left to find a "whoar" for the night, and I wandered off toward the hotel where I was expecting mail and, perhaps, making connections with Beaman.

Beaman had not been seen for several weeks, and the hotel manager told me that he had heard that Beaman had moved elsewhere into the interior. He had no idea whether or not he was still working for the museum. But I did have three letters from home, all from my stepfather, which I immediately read in the hotel lobby. Each was more discouraging than the last, and the most recent urged me to return home immediately. My mother's health had not improved, and the doctor had told my stepfather that nothing could be done for her. The letter ended with an urgent request: "Gregory, please return home as soon as possible. Your mother asks about you every day. I only hope you will not be too late."

But here I was in Panama, completely broke, without a job, and no friends to ask for help. My first reaction was to return to the wharf and attempt to bargain with some ship's captain that might be heading toward Puerto Rico or the Virgin Islands. But by now it was late at night, and I was without a place to sleep. The manager allowed me to sleep in the far corner of the lobby on the floor. I had a terrible time sleeping. Too much was on my mind, and it was my first night away from the ship. I had come to accept the rocking motion of the sea.

I must have slept toward morning, because the manager woke me early and asked me to leave before the owner, who apparently did not appreciate "itinerant sailors," found me there. I wandered down to the dock in search of a ship that could take me home. It took me several hours of talking with various sailors before I was told that a Puerto Rico-bound freighter, the *Crimea*, was due in five or six days, and that it was likely that I could find work. Sailors often jump ship at the first port, and so the ship's officers are always looking for able men.

I found nothing more of interest along the docks, so I walked back into town where I found a small cafe. I spent some of my last money for a cup of coffee and a biscuit. The old waiter, an x-sailor by appearance, looked me over and asked: "Boy, ere ya heden oot soon? Witch ship ya on?"

I quickly explain that I had just returned from the South Seas, but that I had to find a way to St. Croix, where my mother was gravely ill. "I don't have money for passage," I told him, "but I would be willing to work off the expense."

"Woud ya speend a few days heping a friend first,? he asked. "Mr. Wallace is lookin' fer a man to check hes camp. He as me ta watch fer an honest man that wuld hep." He paused a couple seconds, than added: "The pay is good and it wuld take but three-four days."

I immediately asked about further details, but the waiter knew little more. He did add that, "Mr. Wallace eats hair ever day bout one. Ya culd ask em, den." Since it already was close to noon, I decided to wait for Mr. Wallace. If I was forced to wait for the *Crimea*, I would need to work someplace if I wasn't going to starve in the meantime.

At little more than a few seconds after 1 p.m. an elderly, over-weight gentlemen, dressed in a gray suit and carrying a fancy cane, walked into the cafe. He immediate went straight to a booth in the back, without saying a word to the waiter, and squeezed himself in. The waiter brought him a cup of coffee and asked what he would like to eat. Once Mr. Wallace ordered, the waiter pointed in my direction and apparently explained my situation. I could only hear a small part of the conversation, but the waiter soon motioned for me to approach.

"So you require work, eh, young man?" said Mr. Wallace. "Yes, sir, "I answered. I must wait for five or six days for passage to Puerto Rico, and I'm broke."

Mr. Wallace took another sip of coffee, then, looking over his glasses, he told me that he was looking for a man to check on a lumber camp he owned in the Charges River area. "It need only take four days, a day and a half to get there, a day on site, and a day and a half return," he said. "For that I will pay you $25 on your return. And I will also pay for your trip. Are you interested, young man?"

"Yes, I am," I replied. "But, Mr. Wallace, what am I to check on once I get there?"

"Ah, yes," he responded. "You will be expected to ask what has happened to the manager, Ricardo Cruz, who seems to have forgotten to make contact with me in recent weeks. You also will need to see to it that the men are still on the job, and when I can expect the next shipment of lumber." Wallace added, "I want a full account of the situation."

"Mr. Wallace, I am not a lumber man, and have no experience with such an operation. Are you sure that I can properly assess the situation?" I asked.

"Young man, you are perfect for the job," he told me. "Leave as soon as you can. If you will come with me to my office after I eat I will provide you with directions and enough money to pay for your transportation to and from the camp. I will pay you your fee when you return with your report."

I suppose that I should have been suspicious of my assignment once we reached the so-called "office." It was little more than a tiny room in the back of a run down store about two blocks away from the bar. But Mr. Wallace did provide a map and directions, and also gave me $15 for transportation. Five dollars of that, he told me, was to pay Juan Gurerro of Colon, who would take me to the lumber camp up the Charges River.

"If you leave right away, you can reach Colon this evening. I will telephone Senior Gurrero to meet you at the bus station this evening, and you can be in camp by mid-day tomorrow," he told me. With that, he handed me $15, and excused me with, "I wish you well."

I caught one of the Canal Zone buses a few blocks away, and was soon en route to Colon. Once on the bus, I ate the oranges and biscuits that I had purchased with my last few cents. The route followed the Canal and passed several places where Beaman and I had visited while collecting birds. When we stopped at Suzana's village I looked for her, but to no avail. I could not help but wish that she was still available. How I longed for another night of love-making with Suzana. It had been far too long since my affair with Rebecca in Tahiti.

It was after dark when I arrived in Colon, but Senior Guererro was waiting for me. Guererro was of middle age, obviously poor, from the looks of his clothes, and he walked with a significant limp. But he seemed eager to be of assistance.

What was most important was his willingness to leave first thing the following morning. So I accompanied him to his house, where his wife served a wonderful meal, and where I was given a bed for the night. It was after midnight before I fell asleep, and I was awake at first light. But that night was the first night that I had slept straight through for many months. Aboard ship, the coming and going of the sailors rarely allowed me to sleep more than two hours at any one time.

Our route up the Charges River required the use of a small motorboat that Juan had at the ready on the riverbank, about a mile from his house. And it took us until late morning to reach a small village in the interior. We left the boat on the riverbank and walked up the street to a small house that belonged to Juan's wife's cousin, where we were invited to eat. The beans, rice and tortillas tasted wonderful. And after some general conversation about family and friends and what we were about, we climbed on two horses and began the second phase of our journey.

The lumber camp was not more than ten miles distance, but the route would have been impossible without Juan. Numerous side-trails, some more heavily used than the one we followed, were commonplace. The going was also made difficult because of the muddy condition of the trail. It would have been an extremely long afternoon if we had walked. However, in spite of all this, I was impressed with the forest that we passed through. On several occasions I heard bird songs that I recognized as being species that I knew were rare or difficult to find. And many of the birdsongs represented completely new species. I could not help but wonder if Beaman had been able to visit the area.

It was almost dark before we suddenly emerged into a clearing with a few run-down shacks and a huge pile of sawdust. A few dozen logs lay scattered about, and in one corner of the compound was a stack of cut boards that seemed ready for transporting. Behind the pile of boards was a muddy roadway that apparently provided a route to the Canal Zone.

Almost immediately we were surrounded by about a dozen men, all Panamanians dressed in terribly dirty clothes but with a look of relief on their faces. I immediately informed them that I had been sent by Mr. Wallace and wished to see Senior Cruz. But without any further introduction, they began demanding that they be paid. They stood there with outstretched hands. And when I told them that I not brought any money with me, they began cursing me, Juan, and Mr. Wallace. It was an extremely rowdy scene, and I began to realize for the first time how vulnerable we were.

These men, I learned, had not been paid for several months, and they had little remaining food and no transportation. An ancient truck that they used to haul boards had broken down several weeks earlier, and so they remained in camp, waiting for Mr. Wallace or his assistant to appear with their pay. They all thought that I had arrived with their pay. They were all in an extremely ugly mood! I was never given an explanation of Senior Cruz's absence.

One of the men, who seemed to be the group spokesman, and who also carried a pistol tucked into his belt, instructed another man to take our horses to the barn. He then informed us that we were to be confined to one of the buildings, that they would decide what to do in the morning. And we were physically led to one of the shacks, and forced into a room without windows, but with a door that locked from the outside. A guard was posted on the porch.

"Juan," I said, "What are they to do with us? They must know that we are not at fault." I had tried to explain our situation, but the men only got more unruly and threatening, and I was unsure whether they understood any of my explanations or not.

"My cousin was among the men," he answered. "He had motioned me not to acknowledge him when we first arrived. I believe that he will help us."

We were in a very dangerous predicament, what with the mood of the loggers. I was extremely concerned about our safety.

A shot suddenly rang out, somewhere across the compound. But we had no way of knowing what was happening, since we were confined in a room without windows. I tried to find a hole in the rough walls, but it seemed that this room was tighter than any of the others we had seen. It made a great jail.

And when we called to our guard, who was sitting on the porch out of sight, we received only a brisk answer, "You will see."

That night was one of the longest I can remember. There was no bed in the room, only a single chair and an ancient table. From the sounds outside, it appeared that the loggers were involved with some kind of gathering, as we could hear their occasional shouts. We also could smell smoke that we decided was at first from burning wood, and then from cooked meat. The next day we learned that they had killed one of the horses for food, and that they built a huge fire in the center of the compound, where they cooked the horsemeat.

It was mid-morning before we were brought outdoors. We were given our own jug of water that we had brought with us, and a strip of meat from the cooked horse. I had no trouble eating the meat, but Juan could not. He told me later that he could not eat a horse that had been raised by his family. I was able to hide the uneaten meat in my shirt for possible needs at a later time. And soon, in spite of our explanations of the events that brought us to the camp, we were taken back into the room and the door locked behind us.

All during the remainder of the day and that evening we were ignored, without any additional contact with our captures or any additional food. But the loud talking and shouts that night, during which time the loggers were again cooking horsemeat, suggested that they were even more riled up than the previous night.

It was close to midnight when we heard someone at the door. The loggers were still going strong, and it seemed that they were even louder and more obnoxious than they had been earlier in the evening.

"Juan, it is Ramon," came the voice from the door, as it swung open to show a silhouette against the distant firelight. "Come, you must escape now. They have somehow got whiskey, and are talking about killing you to take to Colon so they can demand a ransom for your friend." Ramon had offered to relieve the guard, and had taken that opportunity to free us.

Once in the outer room, we crawled out a side window away from the fire, and ran across the compound toward the protection of the dark forest. "This way," said Ramon. "There is a trail just beyond where we can circle the camp to the old road. That will be our fastest way to safety."

But it was not to be, for apparently the original guard returned too soon and discover that our room was vacant, and he ran back to the fire to report our escape. There was a sudden commotion, with several guns being fired, and orders were barked to search the forest to recapture us. It was obvious that, if we were to remain free, that we could not use the main trails or the logging road. We would need to stay hidden in the forest.

So off we ran as best we could through a maze of shrubs and vines, giving little heed to the possibility of running into a poisonous snake or some other dangerous animal, like a jaguar or mountain lion. It was extremely difficult going, and by the time we stopped to consider our location and which direction we would need to go to reach a village, all three of us were covered with cuts and bruises. We would have made a sorry-looking trio. But we had distanced ourselves from the loggers, so as far as we could figure we were relatively safe.

Ramon had lagged behind, and was limping even more than before. He was in obvious pain, and we knew that if he was going to be able to stay with us that he would need to stop and rest. We stopped to rest. Except for the abundant sounds of the nighttime jungle, we could not detect any of our pursuers. It was a welcome refuge for me, but both Ramon and Juan seemed extremely nervous about being out in the forest in the middle of the night.

It was then, while we sat facing each other in the darkness, that Juan explained that his leg had been broken when a horse had fallen on him high in the mountains, and it had taken him seven days before he reached any help. The village curandero had saved his life, but had been unable to repair his leg.

Ramon seemed to have a reasonably good idea about our location, and suggested that we continue on to the left another hour or so to get further away from the camp and where we would encounter a long ridge that would lead us to a village and safety. That village had family that we could depend upon. Apparently, the Panamanian loggers were mostly from around Panama City, and had few relatives in Colon or along the Charges River.

The additional distance from the logging camp was most difficult for Ramon, but not once did he complain. We finally slept against trees with a small fire between us for about two hours in the early morning. It was surprisingly cool, and the fire was necessary, in spite of the possibility of attracting the loggers. Ramon said that he was reasonably sure that they had all returned to the camp by now. "All of them are too lazy to spend time searching for us. But they will search again in the morning. And they will probably take the remaining horse down the logging road. We must stay away from that route."

The dawn chorus of tropical birds was amazing. I awaken thinking that I was back in the Chiriqi highlands with Lehman's scientists. But my first movement revealed my sores and cuts, bringing me back to reality and the dangers that still confronted us. My companions were already sitting closer to the fire, absorbing what little heat they could. They had let the fire burn down to where it sent out almost no smoke that might attract our captures.

Ramon spoke first. "Only one man at the camp is aware that I have family nearby, and I don't believe that he will inform the others. So it is very unlikely that they will have any idea of our intentions."

Juan added, "If we stay away from the road and the main trails, we can work our way to the village by mid-afternoon. Once there we will be safe."

It appeared very unlikely, no matter how well we did in alluding the loggers that I was not going to be back in Panama City in time to make connections with the *Crimea* for a passage home. My principal concern at this stage was to remain alive.

Our trip through the forest went without a hitch. At no time did we hear or see anything that suggested that we were being hunted. But when we got close to the village, Juan went out into the clearing first. Our thinking was that if the loggers were waiting they would easily recognize Ramon, but probably would be unsure of Juan.

The coast was clear, however, and in no time at all we were welcomed into the home of Thomas Guadalupe, who I soon learned was the local alcalde, with considerable influence in the area. Once we told our story, fresh fish was fried and, along with plenty of beans and tortillas, we were allowed to eat our fill. It was most welcome.

That evening Senior Guadalupe chaired a meeting of about a dozen local townspeople in the local meeting hall where we told about our recent adventure, including the imprisonment, our rescue by Ramon, and our nighttime escape. Senior Guadalupe was elected to represent the village by going to Colon to meet with key government officials. He would request the government to take the necessary steps to close down the logging operation. Several individuals felt strongly that it was an illegal camp anyway, and that this incident finally gave them the opportunity to do something about it.

My main interest, however, was to continue to get back to Panama City as soon as possible. So in the morning, Senior Guadalupe and Juan and I, riding in Guadalupe's horse-drawn buggy, made our way to Colon, arriving at Juan's house by noon. By mid-afternoon I was on a bus en route to Panama City.

The bus trip was longer than the previous trip to Colon, with more stops along the way. So, by the time we arrived in Panama City it was almost daylight. I had slept only between stops. But I was waiting at the cafe when the same waiter opening up that morning. He seemed somewhat surprised to see me. Since I was two days late, I wondered if he and Mr. Wallace thought that I was no longer alive or that I had taken off on my own with the travel money.

I decided not to mention the trouble at the mill to either the waiter or Mr. Wallace, but only to report that Senior Cruz was no longer there and the loggers had complained about not being paid and that they could not transport the boards because the truck was no longer operating. I was mostly interested in obtaining the $25 owed me for his dirty job and finding transportation home.

After a cup of coffee and two biscuits, I walked over to Mr. Wallace's office, only to find a sign on the door that read, "Out of Town." There was nothing more I could do without waiting around in hopes that he might return. So, with about $4 remaining from the original $15, I went back to the docks to see if I might find a ship going to Puerto Rico.

The *Crimea* had passed through the Canal two days earlier, and I found nothing promising. So by early afternoon I returned to the cafe. The waiter had no idea about Mr. Wallace being out of town. "He came in fer supper two days ago," he told me. "I ain't seen 'em since."

After another cup of coffee and a biscuit, I went back to Wallace's office, but found that nothing had changed. However, the store next door was open, so I went in and asked the man there if he had any notion of Mr. Wallace's whereabouts. "None whatsoever," he told me. "And I have no wish to know anything about that man. He is a liar and a cheat."

With that kind of response, I told him about my recent experience with Mr. Wallace and his logging camp. It only brought on another comment about Wallace's character, as being untrustworthy and a cheat. And after a short time, the man asked me if I was an American. When I told him I was, he suggested that I go report my experience to the American Counsel. "Maybe they can assist you in retrieving what is owed you, as well as helping you find transportation home."

The idea of help from the American Counsel was something that I had not even considered before. So suddenly I knew where I must go next. And within a couple hours I had walked across town to the American Embassy. Before entering, I tried to straighten my clothes and hair, so that I would not look so dirty and abused. But I must have been a poor sight, because the lady at the desk immediately called an assistant to come out front.

They listened politely, from a distance, as I explained my predicament. But then they explained that the American Embassy was not in a position to help every American sailor that ended up in Panama. They did check a roster of American ships scheduled to pass through the Canal en route to Puerto Rico, and handed me the names and dates of three ships on which I might try to find work during the next two weeks. With that, the assistant went elsewhere and the lady at the front desk went back to her typing. I was obviously excused.

I walked back out into the warm afternoon sunlight feeling very much alone. I started to walk back to the waterfront when I came upon the British Embassy. Without knowing exactly why, I entered to find a balding man at the front desk reading a book. He looked up and with a friendly smile asked, "Yes, sir, what can I do for you today?"

"I am an American, sir, but received no help at all at the American Embassy. My mother is very ill in the Virgin Islands, and I need to find transportation home." And I continued my story about my experiences since returning from the South Seas. It took me more than 20 minutes, answering a few pertinent questions about the British expedition, before he told me to sit down and he would make an inquiry.

Ten minutes later I was invited into an inner office where I was introduced to an older gentlemen, a Mr. Turner, who immediately told me that he had already instructed an assistant to try to find transportation for me. "In the meantime, young man," he said, "please tells me exactly what arrangements you had made with Mr. Wallace and what you found at the Charges lumber camp." He paused a moment and then, pointed to a lady sitting at an adjacent desk, he added: "I have asked Mrs. Golden to record our conversation. Do you mind?" "Not at all," I answered.

Although I was unsure why the British Embassy was so interested, I again related the details of the arrangements and my arrival and imprisonment in the camp and subsequent escape. Mr. Turner listened intently, making several notes, and asking several questions. Finally, he told me that Mr. Wallace was wanted by the British for fraud and conspiracy. But they had no idea that he was back in town. That certainly helped explain the dingy office, I thought. That conversation lasted for about two hours.

Finally, Mr. Turner excused himself and the lady taking notes, and asked me to remain long enough to read and sign her notes. He returned shortly with the information that his office had contacted the U.S. Navy and located a supply ship that would be passing through the Canal the next morning en route to Puerto Rico. They have agreed to take you on at 8 a.m. if you wish. "You may stay with us overnight, Mr. Stewart, and we can see that you board on time in the morning. Would that be all right with you?"

My mouth must have dropped open with his announcement, because he smiled slightly when I thanked him profusely. He then had another gentleman lead me to a room on the second floor, where I was informed that I could bathe and change into the clothes that had already been laid out on the bed. In closing, he added: "Supper will be served in the dinning room, down the stairs on the left, in one hour."

I could not believe my good luck. Finally, I had a way home. And not from my own countrymen, but from the British. I will never forget that bath, the clean clothes, and wonderful dinner, and the soft bed. I slept like a baby.

Chapter 9

The trip to Puerto Rico went without a hitch. And the very next day I discovered a freighter bound for Fredricksted, St. Croix. So, in less than two weeks after being held captive by the loggers in Panama, I was back on the island where I had grown up. Although the British Embassy had helped me send a cable to my stepfather, telling him that I would be home soon, I wasn't able to let him know the exact date. So, after docking at the Fredricksted Pier, I had to walk the approximately four miles to my parent's home.

It was wonderful to be back on the island that I loved so much, but I arrived with a heavy heart not knowing what to expect. I was even unsure if I would find my mother still alive. She had been gravely ill for several months. But I soon discovered that she was alive, and she was waiting for me. I found her lying on a daybed that had been placed on the front porch so she could enjoy the flowers and birds that were so abundant. As I walked up the front path, she cried out my name, and that brought my stepfather running from inside the house. They both welcomed me home with long hugs.

It was immediately obvious that my mother was not well. She was only a shadow of her formed self, little more than a skeleton. "I expected you today, Gregory," she said. "I am so happy that you are home." My stepfather then told me that she somehow knew when I would arrive, that she had predicted my arrival that very day. And that was the reason that she had insisted that she be taken to the porch to watch for me. Although I didn't make anything of it at the time, I later wondered how my mother could know such things. No other person knew when I would arrive home that day.

It was immediately obvious that she was exhausted from her wait and my arrival, and also from the pain that I learned she suffered continuously. And so, after a short visit, she was taken back to her room, given some medicine, and left to sleep. It was then that I was able to visit with my stepfather. He looked tired and much older from when I had last seen him, almost three years earlier. And the news that he gave me was terrible.

"Dr. Garner told me more than two months ago that she may not have more than another two-three weeks," he said. "I did not tell your mother. But she knows that she doesn't have long. I believe that the thought of you coming home is the one thing that has kept her alive."

"Is there nothing that can be done?" I asked.

"Six months ago, after she was first diagnosed with cancer, Dr. Garner arranged for a Dr. Garza to examine her when he made his monthly visit here from San Juan. I talked with both doctors afterward, and they agreed that it was just a matter of time." My stepfather paused a few seconds before he continued. "I was told that in these cases little can be done. I have tried to keep your mother as comfortable as possible."

"But," I said, "maybe we can take her to New York, or to another doctor."

"I am sorry, Gregory, but it is too late. Dr. Garner explained that we discovered her cancer far too late, after it had affected many parts of her body. He explained that an operation would surely kill her at this stage."

As we talked further it became clear to me that I would need to prepare myself for loosing my mother. It was only a matter of time. And that my time with her more than likely was to be very short.

In retrospect, I guess I already knew the facts. And I decided that night, as I lay there in a bed that I had not slept in for several years, that I would try to keep her spirits up as best I could in the time remaining.

I had not been sleeping more than an hour or two when I was awakened by a loud cry from my mother's room down the hall. The sharp cry came again, and I realized that she was crying out in pain for her medicine. I could hear my stepfather going to her room to comfort her, and after several more cries, she apparently went back to sleep. I learned the next morning that this had been the normal routine for several weeks, each time the strong drugs she was given wore off.

Less than two weeks later she died in her sleep. My stepfather told me that morning that when she did not cry out that night he had gone into her room to check on her, but discovered that she had passed on. He had remained by her bed the rest of the night, coming out only when he heard me stirring in the morning.

Those last two weeks had been extremely hard on us. I had spent as much time as possible with my mother, giving my stepfather a much needed break. But he, too, had spent most of the time she was awake at her side. My mother and I had talked, principally about all the good times we had known before I had gone away to school. At that time I knew that she enjoyed out conversation; she even had laughed about various happenings. She told me numerous times how happy she is that I had come home. She also told me that she was glad for my opportunities to see many parts of the world.

"Gregory," she said, "continue your love of nature. Do not let your friends talk you into taking work you don't want. You are too smart to work in the cane fields. Travel and see more of the world." She paused for a long time, looking at me. Then she added, "There will come a time when you will be needed at home to fight for the natural beauty of the islands. When that time comes, speak out for what you know is right."

Although I do not remember those words having a profound effect on me at the time, I was to remember her advice many times in later years.

My mother's funeral brought out all her many friends and acquaintances. I saw people that she had known all the years she had lived on St. Croix. She truly loved 'my little green island,' as she called it.

I also had the opportunity to see dozens of friends and schoolmates that I had not seen for many years. Afterwards, however, I remember thinking what little I had in common with any of them. It was like I had become a completely different person from the boy who had left St. Croix for New York City.

There was one exception, however. Sonia Harrison had blossomed from a skinny tomboy, who had trailed after me on several hikes, to a full-bosomed woman. She, too, had been away to school in Boston, and had only recently returned to her family. It seems that we had much in common, and we agreed to get together soon to talk about our off-island experiences.

I spent the next several days working around the house, helping my stepfather. He apparently had let things slide around the house and yard during my mother's illness, and it was "now time to get caught-up" he said. He truly drove himself those first several days, and I finally talked with him about his need to get some rest. He had spent too long a time at my mother's side without proper rest, and if he did not ease up soon, he, too, would get sick.

It took two long weeks of working long hours every day about the house and yard before he began to slow down. And it was only then, after supper one evening, they he seemed to give in. We had talked about what still needed to be done when he suddenly came close to collapsing. He sat down in his favorite rocker and put his face in his hands and cried. I was startled at first, because I had never before seen my stepfather cry. And before long he began to tell me how much he loved my mother and how much he was going to miss her. It took him more than an hour before he calmed down, and then he sat there for the longest time, leaning back in his rocker without saying a word.

Finally, after a long silence, he spoke. "Gregory," he said, "we must get on with our lives. I have been offered a job managing a new rum factory near Kingshill, and I believe that I will accept it."

He looked over at me and said, "You are welcome to come with me, or you may wish to find other employment. I have good contacts, and I would be glad to help you find work. Our money is very short, after the medical bills have been paid, and we both must work if we are not going to end up in the poorhouse." After another pause, he added: "I am sorry that I cannot send you away to a university, I know you would do very well. But," and I interrupted him.

"Sir," I said, "I don't expect any further schooling. You have done all that I could probably ask already, by sending me to New York. And," I added, "even if I could, I don't believe that I could manage any additional schooling. My love of nature and my need for adventure is bound to take me elsewhere."

He looked at me for a long time, and then he said, "You know, Gregory, your mother knew you very well. She once told me that you were an adventurer, and that a good part of that was my fault." He chuckled, and then said, "I can only say that I wish you well. But if I can help you in any way while you stay on St. Croix, you know I will do my utmost."

Never did I doubt his good intentions, and I also realized that much of my own personality was due to his nurturing. And I also knew that if he was a few years younger he would have joined me in whatever adventure awaited me.

But I also realized that unless I left the islands and returned to New York or perhaps London, it was going to be extremely difficult to find an expedition that I could join.

Two days later I received an invitation to a birthday party of a casual acquaintance who had attended my mother's funeral, and who I had briefly talked with afterwards. Donald Hardy was to turn 20 the following Saturday, and his folks were giving him a party. At first I decided not to attend, but then I realized that if I was going to find some kind of work, until something better turned up, I had better start making contacts.

The Johansens, the folks I had lived with while attending school in Fredricksted, had also attended my mother's funeral, and they had invited me to come visit and stay with them whenever the opportunity arose. In a sense, they were like second parents. And so I decided that I would ride into town on Saturday morning and stay with them overnight, and to attend the Hardy party that evening.

The Hardys lived on the edge of town in a new large, stately house. Although I had never been inside before, I had no trouble finding it. And the evening was a marvelous success. Not so much due to the several friends that were present, whom I had not seen in years or from the suggestions about possible employment, but Sonia had also been invited. And in spite of the fact that Donald also had eyes for her, it seemed obvious to me, right from the start, that she and I were about to rekindle our friendship.

The very next day I went to church with the Johansens. Although I was not a religious man, I knew that Sonia also attended that Episcopal Church. And sure enough, she was in attendance.

Afterwards I walked her home, and she invited me in to meet her parents. And I even stayed for lunch. It was a most remarkable afternoon. Not since Suzana, in far off Panama, did I experience such a strong feeling for a woman. We were two prodigals who had come together at just the right time. I was to see her several evenings each week for the next several months, and I was to fall madly in love with her.

Work on St. Croix was not easy to find, unless one was willing to work in the sugar cane fields. And the other option of working for my stepfather near Kingshill, where I would need to live, was out of the question once I met Sonia. I strongly wanted to remain near her in Frederiksted.

At Donald Hardy's birthday party, I had also visited with George Severs, someone who I had only casually known before going away to New York. George and I hit it off very well because he also seemed to have a love for nature and adventure, although, except for a few trips to St. Thomas, Puerto Rico, and Dominican Republic, where his father currently ran a sugar cane plantation, he had never been off the island. But I later learned that George had read everything about the natural world that he could get his hands on. George also said that his older brother managed the Lower Love Plantation, the largest of the sugar cane plantations on the island. And when he offered to ask his brother if he could find work for me, I told him that I would be interested only in some kind of management position.

One evening in Fredricksted a few days later, before going to see Sonia, George came to see me at the Johansens. "Greg," he said, "I asked my brother about a job, and he would like to talk with you about how be might best control rats and mongooses. If you are interested, he will be in town tomorrow, and you can talk with him then."

I immediately agreed to see his brother, Jonathan, the next day. I must admit that, at the time, I did not know of any best way to control these two nonnative mammals, but I was aware of the impacts of these two very different creatures. Mongoose populations had exploded on all of the islands where they had been introduced to control rats, and had become a serious concern. Most of the land owners, realizing that the mongoose was not going to control rat populations, were now worried that they might introduce some sort of disease that could affect humans. I was more concerned, however, about their affects on the native wildlife, especially ground-nesting birds and lizards.

George also invited me to go hiking with him the following Saturday. He planned to hike around the northwest end of the island to the top of Hams Bluff, a wild, uninhabited portion of the island. I immediately accepted his invitation, as I had never visited the upper portion of that area before. It would be a great adventure, and I was impressed that someone else had the very same interest in exploring the island as I.

My enthusiasm for the Hams Bluff hike was all but forgotten when I saw Sonia that evening. She wore a print dress that seemed to highlight her marvelous body, and I could barely take my eyes off her. She seemed also to know exactly what effect she had made.

We walked northward along the shore for a long time, talking about her schooling in Boston, and then about my adventures in the South Seas. She was curious about the women in Tahiti, as she told me she had read stories about how open they were to strangers. I did my best to explain their lack of inhibitions without including my personal experiences. But she undoubtedly sensed that I, too, had enjoyed those same inhibitions.

We had walked about a mile out of town and were sitting on the beach, with the wind in our faces and our bodies barely inches apart. "Greg," she said, "I so envy you men who can go off and travel around the world and enjoy the women you encounter. Women here have no such opportunities. We must meet the right man in a proper setting and time before we can even think of such things." She paused, and moved closer to me and put her hand in mine.

After a few more seconds, she added, "I want those same things, Gregory."

I turned toward her and leaned over and kissed her cheek. She then reached over with her free hand, turned my face toward hers, and kissed my lips. It was a long and passionate kiss, and one that quickly aroused me from full control to nearly grabbing her and immediately undressing her and making love. Instead, I continued kissing her, and slowly took my free hand and caressed her back and neck, pulling her even closer and tighter against me. She responded with equal desire.

We sat there making love, fully dressed but knowing that we could have gone further, for an hour of more. Finally, she turned slightly away and said, "I am afraid that I must start back. It's getting late. And my parents will be worried. I told them only that we would be going for a short walk."

I was highly arouse, and had to remain sitting there for several minutes before I could get up and brush the sand off my clothes. Sonia later admitted that she was in a similar condition. And as we started back to Fredricksted, we were holding hands and stopping numerous times to kiss and to hold each other tightly against each other. It was a glorious evening, and by the time we said goodnight at her door, I was again in love.

The very next day I took the bus from Fredricksted to Lower Love Plantation to talk with George's brother about his problem with rats and mongooses. Jonathan was, at once, a likable individual, who explained that he would like to hire me to reduce rats and mongooses in the cane fields if it could be done. He showed me a room behind the office that I could use for the storage of traps and such and whenever I wished could stay overnight. The room contained little more than a cot, a table, and a sink with running water. Although the pay was barely adequate, I quickly accepted. It was the kind of job that interested me as it would allow me to spend time in the outdoors as well as to learn about two animal species that needed additional study. We agreed that I would start the following Monday.

When I got back in Fredricksted that afternoon, I went to the small library to see if they might have any books or reports on rats and mongooses. As I had expected, there was nothing that I did not already know about. In fact, the books that my stepfather had accumulated over the years, that were already accessible to me, offered much more information than any books available in the Fredricksted Library. But, in leaving the library, I discovered Sonia walking along the street with her mother. They had been visiting her father's business, a drygoods store nearby, and were "just walking, enjoying the lovely day," she told me.

I then walked them back to their house, as it was en route to my house, outside of town, and I told them about my new job. I explained that I planned to read all the material that I could before Monday, and that I was going home to do so. Mrs. Harrison asked me to stay for dinner, since it already was very late in the afternoon. And Sonia offered to give me a ride home afterward if I accepted. I immediately did so. I was eager to spend whatever time I could with her.

Supper was excellent, but I was most anxious to be alone with Sonia. And so very soon afterwards, we saddled her mare, and took off toward my home. She rode behind me with her arms holding me tight. By the time we got to the house, I was highly aroused once again, and, on climbing down, we grabbed each other and kissed savagely. I could barely control my passion, and within a very few minutes we had entered the vacant house and were in my room making love.

It was one of those precious moments that will never be forgotten. No matter where I traveled thereafter, that first time with Sonia would haunt me forever.

Saturday's hike to Ham's Bluff with George was another exciting adventure. Leaving our horses tied under a huge cedar-box tree, at the end of the West End Road, we hiked up the steep path toward the lighthouse. The Ham's Bluff lighthouse, perched at the edge of the steep slope overlooking the sea, was one of St. Croix's most outstanding landmarks. It was visible from as far away as St. Thomas, 40 miles to the north.

The vegetation along the route was extremely dense, and it was next to impossible to get off the trail. Most of the plants were short, stunted trees, bent by the strong winds and draped with mosses and an occasional orchid. "That is a Christmas orchid, a species of *Epidendrum*," George told me. "It is far more common in the mountain forest than here on this windswept hillside."

I suddenly realized that I was truly ignorant about the plant life on my own island. Although I had a pretty good understanding about the animal life, including fish, lizards, birds and mammals that lived here, I had never before given much thought to the vegetation on which they mostly depended.

When I expressed my ignorance to George, he immediately began to identify the various trees and shrubs that we passed. Acacia, bush heliotrope and lantana, along with at least three cactuses – Turk's cap, pipe-organ and pricklypear – dominated the area.

"This habitat can best be called thorn scrub," he added. "Thorn scrub is very different than the St. Croix habitats that occur on wetter zones that support rain forest, deciduous forest and thorn woodland habitats," he added. "Add mangroves, ponds, and seashore woodlands, as well as open grasslands, and St. Croix contains a good variety of habitats for an island."

George then made a statement that I remember very well: "Most of the mountain habitats are fairly safe, but many of the mangroves, as well as the coral reefs around the island, are being damaged by human activities."

"I guess I haven't seen any changes yet," I said. "What areas are you talking about?"

"You must see the Salt River Bay mangroves. Development for a marina there has cut that magnificent forest into pieces," he told me. "Salt River Bay is extremely valuable for its seagrass beds, its coral reefs, and the deep, deep submarine canyon beyond. That area contains some of the most wonderful habitats anywhere in the Caribbean." A few minutes later, George added, "Salt River Bay, however, contains more than just natural features. There is where Christopher Columbus, in his second voyage to the New World, had the first ever encounter with the native Carib Indians." And he continued, "The site also contains the ruins of a pre-Columbian burial site and a ceremonial plaza and ballpark built in the 1200s or 1300s, as well as two European fortresses." He paused a few seconds, and then said, "The Dutch constructed a fort on the western point of land overlooking the entrance to Salt River in the mid-1600s; they controlled the area until the end of the century. A total of seven flags have flown over the Columbus landing site: Spanish, English, Dutch, Knights of Malta, French, Danish, and after 1917, United States."

I was amazed! Although I had lived most of my life on St. Croix, only a few miles from Salt River Bay, and visited it on at least three occasions, I had been unaware of its importance to St. Croix and to all of the West Indies.

"I also am told that Krause Lagoon, on the south shore, is scheduled for development. The governor has been talking to oil companies about possibly constructing a refinery in the area."

"How can that be?" I asked. "St. Croix has no oil, why would the governor think that some company would be interested?"

"I don't know for sure," he answered, "but my father heard that the governor is trying to encourage major industry to develop on the island. It would mean many new jobs, and help with the Virgin Island's economy."

"But it would destroy the truly significant resources of Krause Lagoon. That area is too fragile to survive if a refinery was located on its outer edge," I said. "I used to find birds there that could not be found anywhere else on the island. Clapper rails nest there, and ruddy ducks and whistlers, the West Indian whistling-ducks, also live there."

It was during that discussion, as we were sitting and resting from an especially steep climb, that I detected movement atop the dense brush behind

George several feet. I was sure it was a huge lizard, even though I had never before seen such a huge creature on St. Croix. "George," I said, "slowly turn around and look behind you about 30 feet. There on a heavy branch is a huge lizard. It must be an iguana."

George immediately stood up and turned around. My view was partially obscured by brush, but when I moved to the left a few feet I had a much better view. And sure enough, there was a gray-green lizard about three feet long, with a fringe of skin that stood up on its neck. We both stared at it in amazement. "It is a lizard, and look at its size!" George exclaimed.

"It's an iguana," I said. "As a boy, I heard stories about St. Croix once having these lizards. But until today I had never seen one. I really didn't believe what I had heard. But now," I paused, edging even closer for a better look.

What a marvelous creature it was, stretched out on a branch, seemingly half asleep, sunning itself in the open. I continued, "My stepfather told me that iguanas had once been introduced to most of the West Indies by early-day Indians from South America, either Arawaks or Caribs, so they would reproduce and provide a food supply for travelers."

We watched that huge lizard for several more minutes. How I wished that I had a camera, like that used by Mr. Ashley on the *St. Maria*, so that I could document our discovery.

'Maybe we should capture it and take it back alive to prove what we have found," George said. "And then after we take some photographs, we could return it back here," I said. And with that we decided that we would capture it. It seemed so lazy that we were sure that such an effort would not be difficult. And, from my experiences with iguanas in Panama and on the Galapagos, and knowing that they feed on vegetation and are not dangerous to humans, I agreed.

"You stay where you are, moving about some to focus its attention, and I will sneak closer and grab it," I said. With that I began to inch closer, finally getting to a point at the edge of the bush below the iguana, but still about three feet away. I looked for a place in the bush where I could quietly climb though, but my way was blocked not only by dense brush but several climbing cactuses, each armed with long, sharp spines.

It took me several more minutes of finding a way into the brush before I was close enough to attempt to grab the iguana. Instead of making a sudden grab, I very slowly reached toward it. But then, just inches away, my shoulder touched a branch that moved the branch on which the iguana was resting.

And it suddenly, with lighting speed, sprang away and disappeared from view. It was so fast that, in spite of making a quick grab, I came away empty. In doing that my shoulder rammed against one of the cactuses that sent spines deep into my flesh.

For one of the first times in my life, I gave out a line of curses that I had heard so often aboard ship. "My Lord, where did you learn that?" George said, laughing at my predicament. He only stopped when he realized that my shoulder was injured. A few minutes later, as he helped me extract those sharp spines from my shoulder, I told him about my South Seas adventures and about the various sailors that I had lived with for most of a year.

The remainder of the day was without any additional excitement. And although we looked for another iguana all during the remainder of our hike, no others were seen. It appeared that the one individual was all there was. And yet we knew that if one was seen, a larger population was likely. We agreed that we would visit that area again before long, with a net or some other equipment, to capture one of those illusive lizards.

From the top of Ham's Bluff we had an amazing view in all directions. Below us was the deep blue sea and Mt. Eagle and Blue Mountain, the two highest peaks on St. Croix, dominated the island west to east.

On Monday, I rode the bus to Lower Love, taking some clothes, toilet articles, and other materials that I might use in my new job. Jonathan welcomed me and quickly laid out a few guidelines regarding expectation on hours, a budget, and few other essentials. And then he said, "Gregory, I am told by my brother and others that you are a knowledgeable biologist and someone who I can depend on. If anyone can control these two varmints you can. Good luck! Let me know if I can help in any way." With that I was on my own.

Chapter 10

That first day at Lower Love, I rode horseback around the entire plantation, trying to see the extent of the holdings as well as learn whatever I could about the habits of the workers and owners. Two facts seemed important. First, trash heaps that attracted rats were commonplace. Second, the few trees along edges and at scattered sites contained a surprising number of rat nests. From my reading, I had learned that while the introduced mongoose had done its job of killing rats very well at first, the rats soon learned that the mongoose was active only during the daylight hours and that it did not climb trees. A simply solution for the rat's survival, therefore, was simply to construct their nests in the trees, where the mongoose could not reach them, and to remain out of sight during the daytime. After dark they could go about their normal routine with little regard for mongooses.

So, I reasoned, if rats were no longer the mongoose food of choice, what was? And what did the rat's diet consist of? Were they the same? Perhaps, by controlling a food source one could control both species.

Anyway, that was my initial approach to the problem, and so very soon I began an extensive trapping program so that I could examine the stomach contents of each animal that I caught. My trap line extended from one end of the plantation to the other, and I concentrated the smaller rat traps at the scattered trash piles.

I thoroughly enjoyed that experience in the field, checking the traps and taking detailed notes on all of the animals that I encountered. And although I knew the names of most of the trees and shrubs, I also collected a series of plants that I placed in a home-made plant press so that I could ask George to identify them. During those very first days, I realized how well suited I was for such work. And I also recognized how fortunate I was to have work that

I totally enjoyed. At less than 21 years of age, I already had seen much of the world, and I was now a working biologist.

It wasn't long before I had pretty well resolved the first question. Both of these critters fed on almost any kind of fruit and small animals they encountered, from insects to lizards and birds, more or less in that order. Rat stomachs offered a variety of trash and lots of insects. Mongoose stomachs contained a higher percentage of lizard and bird remains. Their principal bird prey included poultry, doves, and pigeons.

At the end of the first month on the job, I gave Jonathan a verbal report on my progress. I suggested first of all that the numerous trash piles on the property be cleaned up to reduce the rats, and that a single dump be established that could be better controlled. I also told him that trapping would continue to eliminate a few rats and mongooses, but if I was to make a real dent in the population it would be necessary to experiment with various poisons. He agreed, but was concerned about the use of poisons around his hunting dogs. I explained that the poisoned bait would be placed out of reach of the dogs and I would monitor the sites constantly. He concurred, and the following day I ordered three kinds of poison from Puerto Rico.

Jonathan's assistant was a Mr. Manuel, a Negro from Antigua, who lived with his family in a small house behind the office. Although Mr. Manuel seemed rather indifferent to my presence, his daughter, Yolanda, who I guessed at 17 or 18, and very well proportioned, appeared far more interested in me and my activities. It was very obvious, right from the start, that she was available. And, if I had not been so thoroughly involved with my work during the daytime, and thought so much of Sonia during my off-hours time, I am sure that I would have taken advantage of the opportunity.

I continued to see Sonia as often as possible, going into town at least one night during the week and also every weekend. Usually on Friday evening I stayed overnight with the Johansens and spent the evening with Sonia. Saturday I would spend at my house, doing various chores necessary to keep things running as best we could without anyone living there full-time. My stepfather came home every other weekend.

Also, on either Tuesday or Wednesday evening when I came into Fredricksted, I usually ate with the Johansens, and then Sonia and I would take a long walk. Actually we would hurry out to my house where we would spend the evening making love. It became a habit that controlled our very existence. As long as I was in town or planning to go to town, I could think of nothing else. Only when I was back at work, trying to study my two subjects, did I think of anything else.

For a few weeks I came to town almost every other night, and on some of those occasions we actually met at the house where we proceeded directly to my bedroom. I found it hard to believe that I was so much in love. After loving each other, I would lay there, examining her wonderful body and looking deep into her violet eyes. And we would murmur to one another about our love, touch each other in all the secret places, and very soon we would be ready to make love all over again.

On one Saturday, several weeks after I had begun my job at Lower Love, George and I took his father's pickup to the East End. We planned to stop at the Great Pond to see what shorebirds might be present there, and also to explore the cactus gardens along the eastern-most edge of the island.

The Great Pond was filled with shorebirds. It was early fall and migrating water birds were passing through by the millions. Wherever we looked were shorebirds. We identified 18 kinds, as well as another 15 species of land birds that were present in the manchineel trees that surrounded the pond. And there also were a handful of soaring birds, such as the huge frigatebirds.

"The sailors call them man-o'-war or hurricane birds," I told George. "They say that they prey on seabird chicks and eggs, like a pirate man-'o- war ship, and they also claim that greatly increased numbers of frigatebirds signify an approaching hurricane."

"I've watched them all my life. Magnificent fliers. I'm told that they are the largest of any known bird," George said.

"I once found a dead, relatively fresh bird that had washed up on Sandy Point. I measured its wingspan at 94 inches. I love to watch them chase down gulls and terns to get them to drop whatever fish they may have caught. They are marvelous fliers for so large a bird. And they can stay airborne for ever. My stepfather told me that they actually sleep while soaring."

"I have seen them catch flying fish in the air, "George added.

The entire day was filled with one observation of interest after another, and I also was able to ask George about an innumerable number of plants that I did not know. I was impressed with his botanical knowledge.

At East End, we hiked the half-mile to the steep rocky point that is considered the eastern-most point of land under the administration of the United States. The deep waters at that end of St. Croix was more Atlantic Ocean than Caribbean Sea, and, more than anywhere on the island, it had a feeling of remoteness.

We sat at the edge for a long time watching the sea and admiring the numerous Turk's cap cactuses that were so commonplace on the steep slopes. Two hummingbird species - green-throated carib and the tiny Antillean crested hummingbird - were seen feeding on the various flowering shrubs. We thoroughly enjoyed their antics.

En route back to Fredricksted that late afternoon, we stopped at Christiansted, where we ate the remains of the food that we had brought with us. Sitting there under the shade of a huge mahogany tree near old Fort Christiansvaern, we talked about our future. I expressed my desire to join another scientific expedition to the tropics, but that I was now uncertain because of my relationship with Sonia.

"You are very lucky, Greg, to have found such a marvelous women," George told me. "I haven't found anyone that I want to build a life with." He paused and, with a twinkled in his eye, added, "Maybe there are too many luscious Negro women about for me too look too hard."

I chuckled at that remark, and then admitted that I too enjoyed an occasional frolic with a Negro. "They are always so eager. And I sometimes wonder if they are borne humping!" We laughed at that, and then George added: "Watching the Cruzan women at a dance can practically drive me insane."

On a more serious note, George told me that his father was urging him to join him in Santo Domingo on Dominican Republic. "It is my only chance to make anything of myself," he said. "I don't have the gift of research like you. If I'm to become successful, I must go into management, and without that training, that would be available from my father, I'm not sure what I would be."

"But George, you are smart and can do anything you wish," I countered. "You certainly know more about the island's plants than anyone else."

"My knowledge of the vegetation is a waste unless there would be some kind of position for me. There is absolutely nothing here for me." He paused a few moments and then added: "I told my father that, if nothing came up on St. Croix, that I would go back to Santa Domingo with him after the first of the year."

"Have you thought about going to college in Florida or elsewhere?" I asked.

"Yes, but we don't have the money. Nor do we have family anywhere that I could stay with. I think that my best bet would be to go to Santa Domingo." A few seconds later, he added: "Maybe you could go with me. My father told me that he was having problems with rats and mongooses in his fields, too. I told him about your work here at Lower Love, and he was most interested."

I was devastated by this news that George might leave St. Croix. He and I had become soul mates, and I would miss him terribly if he were to leave the island.

It was long after dark before we reached Fredricksted, and I decided that, by the time I bathed and dressed, it would be too late to call on Sonia.

I did see her the following day, however, and we spent most of the day with her parents. It was their 25th wedding anniversary, and family and friends had arranged an afternoon picnic to help them celebrate. It was a long afternoon. Sonia and I both wanted to break away and run off and make love. But it was not to be. I stayed overnight with the Johansens, and left early Monday morning for Lower Love.

It was during that first time that I remained at the plantation all week, without going in to Fredricksted, that Yolanda and I began to get acquainted. Although I had noticed her on several occasions, I had never so much as said hello. From the way she watched me, however, I recognized the same kind of attitude in her that I had seen so often in the South Seas women. She was filled with sex and had little or no inhibitions.

I judged her to be totally bored with life, stuck out on the plantation several miles from town and without friends her age. I, naturally, was an interest to her, whether I accepted her or not.

Late Tuesday afternoon, as I sat outside my room, resting from an extra long, hard day of trapping and preparing bait sites, she suddenly appeared at my side.

"Scuse me, sir, but I brout ye a rum drenk. Ye coud use it, I tink. Ye can call me Yolanda," she said as she approached.

"Yolanda, thank you very much," I answered, as I took the drink. "Are you having one, too, or will I be drinking alone?"

"Alredy hat some," she answered with a giggle.

Looking more closely I realized that she may have had quite a few, as she looked a little tipsy. She definitely was in a friendly and inviting mood. She also was extremely well proportioned, a truly voluptuous women, no matter her age. She reeked with desire, giving off the same signal as so many of the South Seas women. "Raw sex," Henny had called it.

I knew at that moment that I wanted Yolanda, but I also realized that my true love was in Fredricksted, and that any involvement with Yolanda could lead to disaster. And yet, as I looked at her obviously eager body, I realized that it was a chance I would take.

That very night we made love on my cot, and I soon realized that, even at her young age, she was a very experienced women. She knew things and did things that I had only dreamed about.

It was not until the following Friday evening that I was able to get back to Fredricksted and Sonia. During dinner at her folk's home, she told me that a three-masted ship had docked at the downtown pier. Mr. Harrison added that a few of the officers had visited his store, and he had learned that it was a British ship called the *Survivor* that was en route to Cuba. I was at once eager to learn more about her and her crew. Maybe she carried one of my associates from the *St. Maria*.

So after dinner, Sonia and I walked into town and down to the pier. Sure enough, there was the *Survivor*, a three-masted barkintine, a very similar ship to the *St. Maria*. I immediately struck up a conversation with one of the sailors, who knew little if anything about the ship's ownership and any of the officers. He had been a last-minute addition. But he told me that the ship carried a scientist, a Dr. Jorgenson, who he pointed out to me. Dr. Jorgenson was at that very moment walking down the plank to go into town.

As soon as Dr. Jorgenson reached the pier, I introduced myself and very briefly told him of my association with the South Seas Expedition. He seemed quite friendly, and so I ask him if the *Survivor* carried any of the scientists that had been on that expedition.

"No, I am afraid not, Mr. Stewart," he answered, "but we are en route to Cuba where we are to collect several Cuban and American scientists. We will then continue on to Venezuela, where we will study the animal life of the Orinoco. It contains one of the most remarkable wildlife habitats found anywhere in the world."

"Do you have an ornithologist?" I asked.

"Indeed we do, Dr. Ronald Jones. But we could always use an experienced preparator who also could assist with various things aboard ship."

"When do you sail?" I asked.

"Monday morning at dawn. If you are interested in joining us, I will need to know tomorrow."

We talked for several more minutes, and then he excused himself and walked on up the street.

When I finally turned to Sonia, who had been standing beside me throughout our conversation, she was obviously upset. She was pale and, and a few tears stood in her violet eyes. Then she said, "Gregory, is that what you want? Do you intend to leave St. Croix for the wilds of Venezuela?"

I stammered through some excuse about how exciting such an adventure might be, but that I would not leave her behind. All the while she watched me carefully, and I believe that, probably for the first time, she recognized that my love for adventure would eventually overcome all commitment that I might make to her or anyone else.

We continued our walk through town, chatting about this and that, and eventually she asked me to take her home. As we parted, I asked if I could see her the next evening, as we had planned, and she quickly agreed. Saturday morning and afternoon was scheduled for a visit to Krause Lagoon with George.

I decided that, at least for now, I would not go to Venezuela. But the urge to visit that part of the world remained.

Krause Lagoon was an amazing area of mangroves and salt ponds, situated along the south shore. We had brought a flat-bottomed boat that would provide easy access into this seldom visited environment. It was the height of the fall bird migration and we were curious about what we might find.

Shorebirds, herons and egrets, and variety of waterfowl were everywhere. Several hundreds ducks flew off the lagoon when we first arrived, flying a great circle to land out of sight in some other secluded location. We also found several of the year-round residents, such as white-cheeked pintails and West Indian whistling-ducks.

On one occasion we encountered a hen pintail with 24 ducklings. "See the pintail with the ducklings," I said. "That hen is tending her own and maybe two or three other broods, while the other hens are away."

The abundant shorebirds were far more skittish than they had been a few weeks earlier at the Great Pond. They fed close to the protection of the mangroves, rarely venturing far from an easy retreat. "There must be a peregrine about," I told George. "See how nervous and careful the shorebirds are today." And then, almost on cue, a peregrine falcon appeared off to the left, and we watched as it swooped down and hit a sandpiper. We were close enough so that we could actually see the feathers explode from the blow. The peregrine made a quick turn in the air, and landed at the dead sandpiper's side, picked it up, and flew off to some perch to consume its prey. It was a marvelous experience to see such an incident. And that one observation was something we talked about long afterwards.

During lunch that day in Krause Lagoon, I told George about my recent experience with Yolanda. He seemed to enjoy my story, and then he told me about some of the Fredricksted Negro women that he had been involved with in recent weeks. "Don't feel guilty about such a thing," he told me. "I'll bet more than most of the white males on the island take advantage of the eager Negro women. They are just soo eager. Why do you think there are so many mulattos about?"

"I guess you are right," I answered. "I even heard last week that my stepfather has moved a housekeeper in with him at Kingshill. I must admit that I can't blame him, but I wonder now how long he has had an involvement with her."

"Greg, although it's is none of my business, but since you asked, his relationship with Mrs. Camaron has been going on for at least a few years. In fact, they have a child, about two years of age, that lives with her."

I must have looked at George like I was crazy. "I had no idea," I said. "I can't believe it. I wonder if my mother knew?"

After a few minutes of silence, George added: "I heard my mother tell my father once about it. She knew your mother from church, and they talked about it. I am sorry. But such things are commonplace on St. Croix."

It may have been, but our discussion was unexpected, and, in spite of it being a 'common' practice', I guess I lost a little respect for my stepfather that day. Never had I dreamed that he could have been unfaithful to my mother.

Saturday evening went as I had hoped. Nothing more was said about my desire to go off on the *Survivor* to Venezuela. But, as we lay there catching our breath after an especially exciting love-making, Sonia became rather quiet. And I could feel her preparing herself for something different. "Greg, my love," she said, "have you thought about marriage?"

I must have frozen with that question. I honestly had not even thought about the long-term commitment of marriage. I guess that I wanted our current relationship to remain as it was forever.

After a few seconds, I answered, "I have, but until I have permanent work and can afford a home and all the comforts you deserve, we must wait."

She remained quiet for a long time. Then, she asked, "Are you looking for other work? What are your plans?" She paused again, and then added: "All my friends are married or about to marry, and I, too, want to marry and have a family."

Her comments seemed almost a threat, and yet I could not blame her in the least. In a few more moments, I responded. "Sonia, I love you will all my heart. And I want us to be together always. But I am still very young, and it will take some time for me to find adequate employment. Please, give me a chance."

In a few more minutes I added, "I will begin to search for other work, but I know of nothing on St. Croix. I can't bear to work indoors. I am an outdoors person, and I must find work of that type."

Since it already was fairly late, we soon dressed and rode back to town, where I left her at her parent's home. Although we held each other tightly before she left, kissing one another and expressing our love, she had been uncharacteristically quiet since our conversation. I went on to the Johansen's for the night.

Although the timing was bad, I was forced to remain at Lower Love all that week. Poisons had arrived and I wanted to experiment by placing poisoned bait out at various locations about the plantation. But that would require constant monitoring, as Jonathan was most concerned about his valuable hunting dogs. I did not want to kill any of those hounds. Besides, I had grown fond of them all myself.

The following Saturday night Sonia seemed to be back to normal. We had a delicious dinner at her folks' house, and then took our Saturday evening walk. Once in my bedroom she was as responsive as any time in the past. We truly loved one another. Sometime later she begin to explore my body, touching every inch of me, and telling me that it all belonged to her. She kissed my lips and neck and shoulders, and continued her loving touches. I lay there breathing deeply, loving her caresses. She continued, telling me that she was fully satisfied, but she wanted only to make me happy. Her touching and kissing continued until, finally I could not control myself, and exploded with utter abandonment. Then she laid on top of me and held me very tight.

Although I continued to see Sonia on weekends, my work at Lower Love kept me busy throughout the week. And two or three nights each week, Yolanda came to my bed. She provided me with nights of wild sex, but never did I stop loving Sonia.

On a Saturday not long after Thanksgiving, George and I returned to Hams Bluff. Our goal was to capture an iguana and bring it back to Fredricksted where it could be photographed. Although we had not been adequately prepared when we first found it, we returned with a noose that I had rigged up on a pole. Mr. Cutter had utilized a similar device for snaring lizards on some of the South Sea islands, and he had let me experiment with it enough so that I had become fairly good at it.

The day was clear and bright, although fairly cool. We walked slowly, watching for an iguana and also taking care that the pole and cord did not get broken or tangled in the dense vegetation. We made our way to the very top of the bluff without seeing a single iguana. And since it was mid-day we sat in a little clearing and ate what little food we had carried with us.

It was then that George talked to me about his plans. "Greg, I have decided to go back to Santo Domingo with my father right after New Years. He has a job for you controlling rats and mongooses if you are interested."

"I am not at all sure that I can leave Sonia," I answered.

"Greg, I believe that you need to know something. Since you are my best friend, I need to tell you something." He looked very serious.

"What?" I said. "What is it? Tell me."

"Are you aware that Donald Hardy has been courting Sonia? He has been seeing her for a few weeks, at least. And I know that he has had supper at her home on at least two occasions."

I could hardly believe it. "Are you sure?" I asked. "I didn't know." I must have looked shocked, because George quickly added, "They may only be friends. I know of nothing more other than those visits."

"Thank you for saying something, George. I will ask her about it." I was surprised by my strong emotions. I found it hard to believe that she was seeing someone else. But nothing more was said about that the rest of the day.

Soon afterwards, we did spot two iguanas. The first was too far away to make any attempts at capturing it. The second individual was only about ten feet off the trail, and although I made a serious attempt to snare it, it keep just out of range, moving away as the noose was just about in place. In retrospect, I was too upset about Sonia's possible involvement with Donald Hardy to capture such an illusive creature.

"Greg," George said with a laugh, "our problem is that we need to be smarter than the iguana." It was a good attempt to excuse my technique, and we vowed that we would try it again at a later time. But, George and I never again hiked to Hams Bluff together.

That night at supper, I could not detect anything that even remotely suggested that Donald Hardy was anything more than a casual acquaintance. And I decided that I would not say anything about it.

Later that evening at my house, after we made love and were lying there talking about my work and whatever else came into our minds, she got very quiet. Then after a long pause, in which neither of us said anything, she turned on her side and said, "Gregory, I need to tell you something. You need to hear it from me, before someone else tells you."

I looked at her, sensing what she was about to tell me. She continued, "Donald Hardy has asked me to go with him to the New Year's Ball. I have decided to go. He has come to visit me several times, and although I love only you, I realize that our relationship will not go any further. I don't think you are the marrying type. And I want that."

She stopped and we looked at each other for a long time. Finally, she added, "I love you, Gregory. You know that. I could not make love with you like this unless I did."

"But you know that I love you, too," I said. "Can't you give it a little more time?"

Tears formed in her eyes. "I have talked with my parents about us. They know that I love you. But they also think that you may leave any time for more adventure. I just can't stand the idea that you don't want to marry me." With that she burst out crying, burying her face in my shoulder. I tried to calm her down, but it was impossible. I just held her tight, caressing her back and neck. As much as I hated to admit it, I almost agreed with her.

It took more than an hour to calm her down, and then perhaps it was only due to her desire. She climbed on top of me and we kissed long and hard for several minutes. Then, we made love again for what was to be out last time.

As we said goodnight at her door, she begin crying again. As she looked at me I could see that she was trembling. Then she said, "Since I told you about Donald, you have not asked me to marry you. I had so hoped that you would." She shuddered and said, "I can't see you any more, Gregory. Please let me go on with my life." And with that she broke away, opened her door, and disappeared inside.

I stood there, dumbfounded that we were through. I didn't know what to do. I was sure that I loved her, but for some reason I could not ask her to marry me. I wandered back to my room at the Johansens, where I lay awake for several hours, trying to decide what I should do.

I awoke at dawn like any normal day. But it was not any normal day. I had a great burning hole inside of me, part lonesome, part melancholy, and part sickness. Christmas was but two weeks off, and I already had made plans for spending it was Sonia. I was buying an expensive brooch that she had admired in one of the stores. And I was going to give it to her on Christmas Eve. But now, all of those hopes had been destroyed the night before.

If I went to her and asked her to marry me, I knew that she would say yes. And we undoubtedly would have lived a good life, with kids and family. But I was just not ready. It took me an hour or more, lying there thinking about the situation, before I knew what I would do.

That afternoon, I went over to George's house and talked with him about the situation. I told him what had happened and that I was interested in going to Santo Domingo with him and his father. He seemed glad that I was going to join him, but he also was saddened, genuinely, that I was broken up with Sonia.

Afterwards, I took the bus to Kingshill to talk with my stepfather. He lived in a small house behind the Great House, and he was at home. But he was startled to see me.

"Gregory," he said, "what are you doing here? Come in. Is anything wrong?"

I explained my predicament, including my long-standing relationship with Sonia, and that I had decided to join George and his father in Santo Domingo.

We talked for an hour or more about my situation and plans. And finally, after lunch, he introduced me Mrs. Camaron. He told me that they were indeed living together. "I hope you understand, Gregory," he said. "We have been friends for many years, and we have a very good understanding. It does not take away from the love I had and always will have for your mother."

"I do understand, Sir," I answered. "I can only hope that you are happy."

It was a good afternoon and evening. We visited the rum mill and he told me about his work. He seemed to be enjoying it very much. And from comments by his employees, I could see that he was well-liked and, undoubtedly, doing a fine job. That was exactly what I would have expected.

I stayed with him and Mrs. Cameron that night, and left on the early bus to Lower Love the following morning. My next step was to inform Jonathan about my plans to leave his employment and St. Croix.

Chapter 11

I had never before been to the Dominican Republic. Arriving by sea, it was obvious that the island of Hispaniola was larger than my tiny island of St. Croix, and impressive mountains dominated the interior. "The central mountain range, the Cordillera Central, contain some of the highest peaks found anywhere in the West Indies," Mr. Severs told us. He added that "Pico Duerto is more than 10,000 feet in elevation, and Lago Enriquillo, in the west, actually lies below sea-level." He also mentioned that the Island of Hispanola is second in size only to Cuba in the Caribbean, and added that "The island's northern shores are bound by the Atlantic Ocean and the southern shores by the milder Caribbean Sea." He provided us with a wonderful description of the country as we approached Santo Domingo. I had a better understanding about why Hispaniola had such a high diversity of wildlife.

The city itself was very old. It was originally established by Christopher Columbus, and is considered the oldest colonial city in the New World. And I was to learn that many of the old structures still existed. The city reminded me somewhat of what I remembered about San Juan, Puerto Rico. Although I had been too young to appreciate San Juan when I had lived there, I realized very soon that Santo Domingo contained all of the amenities of a large city.

Mr. Severs' assistant, a Mr. Hunt, was waiting for us when we docked, and we soon were en route to the Jordon Plantation, northwest of the city approximately 40 miles. Once out into the countryside, the scene looked very much like that on St. Croix, with the exception of the high mountain background. Sugar cane fields dominated the valleys.

In about two hours we entered the Jordon Plantation, and soon afterwards arrived at the Jordon Great House, where we were to stay. It was an enormous structure, located in about the center of the 1800-acre plantation. The Great House contained 16 rooms, with eight rooms downstairs, including a large central dining room and four full bedrooms, and six bedrooms and two bathrooms upstairs. Mr. Sever, Mr. Hunt, and Senor Jordon's daughter occupied three bedrooms. The fourth was used as a guest room, but Mr. Severs explained that George and I could use it, at least temporarily.

A secondary structure behind the Great House contained four rooms, each with an outside entrance, and one of which I was told would be prepared for my office. It was large enough for a bunk bed that George and I could utilize when guests were using the guest bedroom in the Great House. George was to work with his father and share the main, large office. One of the additional large rooms was utilized by three assistants, who were responsible for various secretarial activities. The fourth room belonged to Mrs. Hernandez, the plantation cook and caretaker.

That first afternoon, after unloading our gear, George and I were given a quick tour of the quarters and offices. My office was large but with few essentials. Mr. Severs explained that he had not learned that I had decided to accept his invitation to work until he had arrived on St. Croix for the holidays. So he told me to set up my office as I pleased. He encouraged me to purchase whatever supplies I might need.

"We can discuss a budget during the next few days, after you have seen our fields," he said. "Please use your own judgement on what you will need. You will find that Santo Domingo has a rather complete stock of office equipment as well as traps and poisons that you might need. You are welcome to use one of the vehicles not being used."

The next room on our tour was the office that was utilized by the secretaries. Although I was introduced to all three, I remember only Ramona. She was one of the most beautiful women I had ever seen. Tall and stately, with high cheek bones and large, dark eyes, it seemed that she could literally look into my soul. I stared at her for a full minute when introduced before I mumbled, "I'm pleased to meet you."

She smiled, as if she was well aware of her effect on men, and then she said, "I am so very glad to make your acquaintance."

Suddenly, I realized that she was Spanish, and probably well-bred. She was very different than any of the women I had ever encountered anywhere else. I become a little more composed when Mr. Severs explained, "Ramona is the daughter of Senor Jordon, the owner of the plantation. She recently returned from Seville, where she attended the university. She is working with us to learn about the business side of the sugar cane operations. And we are very pleased to have her."

Almost from the moment I laid eyes on her, I wanted to know her better. And yet, when Mr. Severs explained her situation, as we walked back to the Great House, I became leery. "Mr. Jordon is extremely protective of his daughter," he said. "She only recently turned 21, and she has been raised within the upper society of Santo Domingo. I am told that she returned from Spain early, before she finished her schooling, because she got involved with someone that her father decided did not fit his image of who she should marry. I also am told that her father is making arrangements for her to marry a young man from one of the better families in the city."

That night, I lay in bed for a long time, thinking about both Sonia and Ramona. I missed Sonia terribly, I sometimes ached for her body next to mine, and I truly missed the wonderful relationship that we once had. I was terribly jealous of Donald Hardy. The idea of the two of them making love was almost more than I could stand. But Ramona was one incredible woman. I wondered if she was aware of the arrangements her father was making for her to marry. Did she even know the man?

I finally drifted off to sleep, wondering how I could somehow get acquainted with Ramona.

The next several days were busy ones, getting to know the Jordon Plantation and my new environment. The sugar cane fields were similar to sugar cane fields everywhere. But each section was lined with tall royal palms, and several of these contained a huge jumble of sticks located near the top. At first I assumed they were hawk nests, but there were too many. Then I wondered if they could possibly be rat nests, but they were three to four times the size of any rat nest that I had even seen. The mystery was solved when I observed an active nest with several palmchats sitting on and around the nest.

Blackbird-size, palmchats are colonial nesting birds that build huge stick nests containing several apartments. As many as a dozen pairs may utilize the larger nests that they construct with thousands of pencil-sized twigs broken off of whatever trees might be in the vicinity. Occasionally, a pair of Antillean grackles will also use one of the apartments.

On the far side of the plantation, at the edge of the foothills, I discovered a free-flowing stream that passed through an area that looked like an undisturbed forest. Since it was lunch-time, I walked into that wooded area to where I found a lovely glade along the stream. A truly wonderful place! And as I sat alone enjoying the greenery of that isolated spot, it suddenly came alive with birds. They apparently had stopping singing and moving about when I entered, but within only a few minutes after I was quiet, they resumed their activities.

Within less than an hour I found ten species that I had never seen before, except as study skins at the American Museum. Most impressive were the Hispaniolan lizard-cuckoo, Antillean mango, Hispaniolan emerald, Hispaniolan trogon, and broad-billed tody. And as I came out of the forest, a huge flock of Hispaniolan parrots flew overhead. Almost all of these birds were endemics, species that are found nowhere else than on Hispaniola. From that first morning on, I knew that I was going to enjoy my new surroundings immensely.

That evening I told George about finding the undisturbed forest, and he was as excited as I. In fact, he wanted to see my streamside forest immediately. However, by the time we had finished supper and I had talked with Mr. Severs about my impressions about what could be done to control rats and mongooses on the plantation, it was almost dark. We postponed our visit to the coming weekend.

George also had some news. He had met one of the secretary's stepsons, Jona Guzman, who worked for a logging company in the mountains near Constanza, about 90 miles distance from the plantation. Jona was taking a few days off to visit his parents.

He said: "Jona told me that the mountain peaks near Constanza get over 10,000 feet in elevation. The uplands contain an extensive pine forest, and there are several bird species there that never get into the lowlands. He invited us to visit him sometime."

"I would love to see the high mountains," I responded. "Maybe we can take a weekend and explore that area. Wow! The sooner the better."

I took two more days exploring the plantation, recording sites that would need to be cleaned up and counting the number of active rat nests in the trees. From what I could see, the Jordon Plantation was very similar to the Lower Love Plantation on St. Croix.

The next morning, instead of going into the field, I planned to go into Santo Domingo to purchase some office equipment, additional traps, and some poison. I had told Mr. Severs about my intentions the previous evening, and he instructed me to get the necessary money in the office in the morning. He also told me to check with the office staff in case anyone needed any additional supplies.

By morning there had been a slight change of plans. Mr. Severs informed me that both he and Ramona would also be going into the city. Ramona's mother, who had been ill for several weeks, had taken a turn for the worse; Ramona would need to leave immediately. So, within the hour the three of us were en route to Santo Domingo.

During the two-hour trip, I learned very little about Ramona. She was obviously worried about her mother. So, when we entered the city, we continued directly to the Jordon home, which was located within the south-central portion of the city. It was a massive structure on a slight rise, overlooking the sea. The gardens surrounding the house were magnificent.

We continued up the driveway to the house, where a servant greeted us and invited us inside for coffee. Ramona went directly upstairs to her mother's room. In about ten minutes, Senor Jordon, himself, appeared. He apologized for not greeting us when we arrived, and he explained that Senora Jordon was gravely ill. "Doctor Gonzales has warned me that she is dying. It was very important that she see Ramona. I thank you for bringing her home."

We remained only until we had finished our coffee, and then we left to complete our business in the city. In driving away, I asked Mr. Severs about the Jordon family.

"Senor Jordon inherited the mansion as well as the plantation from his father. Apparently, it is old money from Spain. The older son has returned to Spain. He did not want to get into the sugar cane business. That is when I was hired. There also is a younger sister, currently going to the University of Seville. But I suspect that Mr. Jordon would like Ramona to learn the business and take over when he dies."

"Then she will inherit the estate?" I asked.

"I imagine so. Thomas, the son, has cut off all ties to the family." He paused a few minutes and added, "It will be interesting to see if he comes home when the Senora passes away. The one time that I met him, he seemed far more interested in parties and the ladies than in his family's affairs. He left for Spain soon afterwards."

That day in Santo Domingo was filled with new experiences. Not only did I see the inside of the largest and grandest home I could imagine, but, with Mr. Severs as my guide, we drove about the city, visiting a dozen or more stores to purchase equipment and supplies. I was especially impressed with the large number of huge stone buildings, especially the Cathedral and the Grand Palace of Columbus. And we spent an hour or more at the Central Market, a huge area where one could buy anything imaginable. And where we also ate lunch.

It was late afternoon before we returned to the Jordon Plantation. And by the time George and I had unloaded the truck and ate supper, it was late in the evening.

Senora Jordon died two days later. Since most of the plantation employees had worked for the Jordons for many years, everyone was given two days off. Mr. Severs was obligated to attend the funeral and he invited me to attend as well. Although George did go with his father, I declined, not because I would not be accepted but because I did not have the proper clothes to attend such an affair.

Instead, I decided that I would spend the day establishing a trap line and to visit the forest that I had discovered a few days earlier. The forest glade was just as it had been on my previous visit, and I sat on the ground for an hour or more, quietly observing the wildlife around me. A pair of black-crowned palm-tanagers came to within a few feet of me as they chased one another around the glade. Then suddenly, I noticed movement near the base of a woody thicket just across the stream. And a few seconds later I was watching one of the tiniest woodpeckers I had ever seen. I knew immediately what it was, an Antillean piculet. Its greenish-brown back, yellow crown, and whitish underparts streaked with black were obvious with my binoculars. But never had I seen such a tiny woodpecker. I couldn't help but wonder how such a creature evolved. It suddenly startled me with a loud and rapid call, like "kuk-ki-ki-ki-ke-ke-ku-kuk." What a marvelous creature!

Since it was still early in the day, I decided to explore the area, and soon found a trail along the riverbank. The route was mild at first, but it got steeper as it ascended the slope. The stream reminded me so much of a smaller version of Monkey River on Gorgona. In about two miles the trail topped out on a long bench that had been partially cleared for crops. And just beyond the small field was a house, built of stones and roofed with palm fronds. Two people, both women, stood in front of the house, cooking on a small fire.

I turned to leave, to melt back into the forest, when one of the women called out, "Senor, you are welcome. Come closer."

"Hello," I said, as I walked over to the fire. "I am sorry for disturbing you. I work at the plantation, and was simply following the lovely stream."

I was close enough now to see that I was talking to a mother and her daughter. The daughter was about 16 or 17 years old, very pregnant and extremely shy. The mother, who I guessed to be 35 at the oldest, was most gracious, and offered me food. I had left my pack with food at the glade, and I had not eaten anything since breakfast. So I readily accepted her offer of a tortilla and beans.

"If you wish to wait, stew will be ready in another hour," she said.

"Thank you, no. The burrito is excellent." After a few minutes, I asked: "Do you ladies live here alone and farm?"

"No, Senor," the mother answered, "Margarita's husband is a goat-herder, and he is with the goats. He returns each evening. It is his milpa. You may call me Mariana."

I remained for only another hour, visiting with Mariana, before I started back down the trail. But in leaving, Mariana called out, "Please wait, senor, I will walk down the trail with you. I must check my kalaloo traps."

And so we left Margarita at the fire and walked down the trail. In about a mile she pointed to a little side-trail that stopped at the stream. A trap built of twigs and wire, and weighed down with stones, was situated underwater a few feet from the bank. Mariana immediately waded into the shallow water to retrieve the trap. It was only then that I became aware of her body that was wonderfully proportioned. She made no effort to hide her breasts that practically fell out of her very sheer blouse when she bent to pick up the trap.

I must have been staring at her in admiration, because she suddenly looked up at me and grinned. "Ha, yes," she exclaimed. "We will have kalaloo tonight. The stew can wait until morning." As she approached I could see that, sure enough, the trap held three fresh-water crabs, five to eight inches in diameter. "They will make a fine supper," I said.

Mariana then looked at me very carefully, and said, "I see you like me. I have not had a man for several months. If you want me, I am very willing."

And without any more thought or conversation, we immediately made love on the moss-covered stream bank. Both of us had been without for too long, and that serendipitous sex was wonderful. Afterwards we lay there for only a few minutes. Then she got up and said, "I hope that I have not embarrassed you, Gregory. I was too eager. I must stay with my daughter to help her with her baby. I am a lonesome woman. You are welcome to visit anytime."

Walking back to the Great House that afternoon, I had no inclination to visit Mariana again. But over the next several months she and I satisfied our sexual needs on numerous occasions.

It was more than two weeks later when Mr. Severs informed me that I was to drive into town and pick up Ramona the following morning. "I am meeting with some officials in the morning, and cannot leave. Since you have been to the Jordon Mansion before, you will know how to get there."

That night I dreamed that I was making love to Ramona. And just as we were about to consummate our love, Senor Jordon appeared out of nowhere. He was armed. I was suddenly wide awake and sweating profusely. It took considerable time to calm down and go back to sleep.

In the morning, I had little problem finding the Jordon Mansion. I was invited inside for coffee, with Ramona as my host. Senor Jordon had already left for his office. But Ramona looked more beautiful than ever, and I could hardly find the words to express my sorrow for her loss. She thanked me, but then said, "You are very kind, Gregory. I am told that you lost your mother a short time ago. I am sorry. Perhaps we can share our grief."

We did share our experiences en route back to the plantation that day. Ramona explained that her mother had been ill with a bad heart for many months, and she knew that it was just a matter of time. "But when she finally passed on, I was very sad. Even though I realized that she would never had gotten well again."

I told Ramona about how my mother had held off her death until after I had returned from Panama, and how grateful I was that I had the opportunity to visit with her before she died.

"Momma knew I was there, but she was too sick to talk at the end. I spent a great deal of time holding her hand. I know that she was grateful."

After a time, I asked if her brother had come home for the funeral. She told me that he had not arrived in time, but that he was in France at the time and had not received the news until afterwards. "He cabled father that he would be returning soon. He loved mother a great deal. Thomas and father had a falling-out when he declined father's offer to take over the sugar cane business."

After a few minutes, she added: "There were other reasons. Father has a mistress. When Thomas found out, he confronted my father, and they had a very bad argument. Not that Thomas is so pure. He had several girlfriends around the city. Only we girls are expected to be celibate until marriage."

I could tell that she wanted to say more, but thought better of it. After a while, she asked: "Gregory, you are the age to marry. Have you not found the right women?"

"On St. Croix, I did have a relationship with a woman. But she wanted to get married right away and have children. I was not ready. Or, perhaps, I had not found the right woman. But I do want a permanent relationship with the right woman."

"What do you think about married men having mistresses?" she asked.

Hardly knowing how to answer, I finally said, "I would hope that my wife would provide me with all that I would need. It is not right, and yet I also have learned that the majority of West Indian men have mistresses. Not long ago I learned that even my own stepfather had a mistress and even a child for many years, even while married to my mother."

"I believe that any man I married would never need a mistress. I would provide all the intimacy he could possibly want."

"I commend you for your attitude. I would appreciate that kind of wife."

There was a long pause, and then she added: "I have one major concern. I am still a virgin, so I do not know if I am capable of satisfying a husband. I came very close to loosing my virginity in Spain. But my father forced me to return home before I had that experience. I am now without anyone to learn from. And being forced to live on the plantation to learn the sugar cane business, which I do not care about, I feel trapped."

Since we were just approaching the plantation, I decided that I had best not respond to her comments. But I knew that sooner or later I would make love to Ramona.

That night I told George all about my conversation with Ramona, swearing him to secrecy. He was greatly surprised that Ramona had discussed such personal things with me, and he told me, "Greg, you have a peculiar quality about you. It appears that women are attracted to you, probably because they think you can be trusted. But," he added, "I have no idea what to advise you about Ramona. Personally, I would love to take her to my bed."

It was several weekends later before George and I were able to take off three consecutive days for a trip to visit Jona in the mountains above Constanza. We rode a bus from Piedra Blanca to Constanza, where Jona met us and transported us by truck about ten miles beyond into the higher mountains. The entire trip, that progressed from about 1,000 feet to about 9,500 feet elevation, provided a marvelous perspective on the changes in habitats. And the temperatures changed as well, from warm and humid conditions in the valley to very pleasant at mid-elevations to quite cool in the highlands. The highlight of the trip, as far as I was concerned, was a wonderful look at a bay-breasted lizard-cuckoo, as it flew across the roadway in front of the truck. Its all chestnut-colored underparts were very different than the slightly smaller gray-breasted Hispaniolan lizard-cuckoo I had seen in my forest glade several weeks earlier.

My only previous experience in an isolated logging camp was in Panama, and I did not want a similar episode. But I was pleasantly surprised at how well-run Jona's camp seemed to be, in spite of the great clearing around the camp and the adjacent pile of equipment and parts. Jona, who I liked immediately, was the assistant manager, responsible for finding and retrieving logs. And so he knew the surrounding mountains extremely well.

That first evening we hiked to a nearby mountain top from where we had an amazing view in all directions. Jona pointed out a higher peak to the north, where he planned to take us by horseback the following day. Our perch high in the Cordillera Central reminded me of the Chiriqi highlands in Panama, and so I told George and Jona about my adventures with the Lehman Expedition. Later, as we were hiking back to the camp, George told me, "Greg, I truly admire your story-telling ability. I was just as fascinated about your Chiriqui adventure this time as when you told me about it more than a year ago. I wish that I had such ability. No wonder you are such a lady's man."

I had never before thought that I was a good storyteller, at least not any better than anybody else. But thinking back, I realized that I could attract attention with my storytelling. Maybe, someday I would even try to put my various experiences into writing.

It was during our trip into the highlands of Dominican Republic that I realized that I had fallen in love with Ramona, probably for the very time truly in love. I missed her terribly, and discovered that I was seriously thinking about marriage. That idea stayed with me constantly, and no matter what occurred those few days that I was enjoying the Dominican highlands, I constantly returned to my love of Ramona. Eventually I told George about my feelings for Ramona, and his only response was that he would be most happy and supportive for whatever I decided.

Chapter 12

My return to St. Croix with a wife surprised everyone I knew. One friend I met on the street told me that he was "more than surprised." He said "I thought that you were a confirmed bachelor, and too much of an adventurer to ever be confined to one place and one woman." My stepfather, however, seemed truly pleased, and Ramona and I were invited to live with him. He still lived in the home of my youth and it seemed very comfortable to being back at home. There was plenty of room, and Ramona seemed very happy there. But I became restless and missed the adventures that might be available elsewhere.

During the next several weeks, however, I looked about the island for some job that might be available. But I could not find anything that attracted my interest. And then, only a couple months after settling in at Fredricksted, my stepfather suddenly became ill and died. It was a complete surprise; he seemed very healthy and so happy about my return to St. Croix. I did not understand what had occurred, but Dr. Garner thought it most likely was a heart attack. I had not seen any indication of this in the past, but my stepfather was likely to have ignored any possible medical problem he might have had. Although my mother had gone to Dr. Garner on occasion, my stepfather did not like to go to a doctor.

His funeral was held in Fredricksted; he was buried alongside my mother. I was amazed at the great number of friends and acquaintances that attended. I knew that I would miss him as he had not only been my father while growing up, supported me through my education in both St. Croix and in New York, but had taught me all that I knew about the natural world, from wildlife to the stars in the heavens.

I again looked for work on St. Croix, but could find nothing that suited me. So I spent considerable time along the Fredricksted wharf, admiring the various ships that docked there. It wasn't long before I discovered that one of the ships was en route to Venezuela on a scientific expedition under the auspices of the American Museum. I was immediately interested. That was the kind of work that I could be excited about, so I talked with the captain, a mister Jennings, about joining the expedition. He informed me that his crew was already filled, and that he had no more room. But in a few days, while the crew was in town buying supplies, I was able to see him again and I expressed my desire to join the expedition. I offered to help in any way necessary, and when I said that I would not require a salary, he finally agreed. We left two days later. I was highly excited about any adventure in a new land that might lie ahead. Although Ramona was not at all happy about my decision to leave her on St. Croix, where she had no relatives or longtime friends, she protested very little. And soon after I left for Venezuela, she returned to her family in Santo Domingo.

We landed in Venezuela on the Peninsula of Paria, a long narrow peninsula running east and west, along an enormous gulf across from Trinidad. I learned that the Peninsula of Paria claimed historic recognition as the first site where Christopher Columbus landed on his first voyage to the New World. For a place to stay, we were offered the facilities of an old cocoa plantation. The owners no longer lived there, but they had been extremely wealthy and had built a magnificent house with plenty of room for our contingent. And they had continued to maintain the house and gardens in superb condition.

Plus, the surrounding environment was amazing. Jungle abutted the beautiful coastal beaches and the mountains formed a green background that was most intriguing. Venezuela's mountain ranges, the Cordilleras de Venezuela, rise to more than 16,000 feet at the summit of Bolivar Peak. Although I was never able to climb the upper peaks, I did visit a number of mid-elevation areas where I discovered dozens of lakes. The largest of these was Lago de Guanoco, a deep blue and quiet body of water surrounded by bright green jungle. And I found the wildlife abundant throughout the entire region. Most amazing were the thousands of butterflies I encountered wherever I roamed; never before had I realized the diversity of these gorgeous insects.

Our accommodations was located a few miles inland but still accessible to the coastal habitats. The Peninsula was a huge fan-shaped landmass with numerous streams and an abundance of wetlands. The coastline was dominated with fine-sand beaches and edged with massive mangrove forests. And the huge house provided all of our needs.

We had a Chinese cook, Su Chow, that we had picked up in Trinidad. Although he seemed very nice, he didn't speak much English, yet he was a very good cook and had our meals on time. And one morning when we got up and the breakfast was warming in the kitchen, we couldn't find him. We yelled and screamed, looked all around, but still could not find him. Finally in a little room where saddles and stuff were kept, we found our Chinaman. He had hung himself. He had jumped off a small stool with his feet almost reaching the ground.

We then notified the authorities who came out from town and asked us a lot of questions. Su Chow was an alien, and that brought up a lot of speculation. We eventually decided that the principal reason for his suicide was because he was lonesome and could not accept his position among so many scientists. That evening we dug a deep hole among the palm trees near the beach and buried him. Although we did not know what his religion might have been, one Christian member of our party did say a few words.

The longer I stayed in Venezuela the more I loved the country. We were on the Orinoco Delta and bird life was amazing, including Orinoco geese and Jabiru storks. The storks stood six feet tall, and I was told that one could split a man's head open in one lick of its bill. And I had never before seen so many ducks. When disturbed, they rose up in clouds that practically covered the sun. All during my stay I collected birds and prepared them as study skins that eventually became a significant collection that was donated to the American Museum.

The major problem during our stay in Venezuela was the nearby activities relating to the First World War. These war-time activities affected the entire region. There was a German wolf pack stationed off Martinique, and the French supplied the Germans with food. German subs would steam off Trinidad and wait for tankers going to Europe. They sank them one after the other like sitting ducks. When the tankers were shut down the oil fields stopped producing oil. But very soon afterwards the oil companies began using conveys where several tankers, accompanied by American and British destroyers, would collect in Port-of-Spain and leave in a pack. God help the German submariners that came near. Our scientists eventually decided it was too dangerous to remain on site and pulled out.

With all that was going on near the Orinoco Delta region, I moved to Guiria, a beautiful place overlooking the Gulf of Paria. I could see Trinadad about 30 miles across the bay. I had a house to myself on a bluff, and I could continue to study the birds and the environment, and I continued to collect.

I had been there only about six weeks when I met a gentleman, a Mister Conway, who worked for the Rubber Development Association, with headquarters in Miami. He was very interested in the area and what I had been doing in Venezuela. We talked on several occasions and I discovered that he was very knowledgeable about rubber development. And when he told me that a team from the Association was heading to the Amazon to look for rubber, I told him that I would be interested in going along. It was to be an enormous expedition where money didn't mean a thing. Knowing about my background and the fact that I spoke Spanish, I was hired. But I would need to report to Manaus where I would be signed up to work.

The only rubber in the world at that time was in Malaya and acquiring that rubber cost America a thousand dollars a pound. To keep our rolling stock viable, including the millions of vehicles on the road, along with the military, we had to find rubber. The Amazon was the original source of wild rubber. So the Rubber Development Association sent me to Brazil's capital city of Manaus, a thousand miles from the sea.

To reach Manaus, I had to take one of the river steamers, up the Amazon River. I learned that the *S. S. Florida* was leaving for Manaus in two days, and I also learned that passengers were allotted ten berths. But when I tried to get a cabin, they told me at the steamship office, that due to the many people that were returning home from a nearby fiesta, this would be impossible. It took considerable discussion and a bit of bribing before I was finally issued a ticket and a cabin.

Arriving on board, I found that my cabin was already occupied. The gentleman occupant informed me that he had "paid extra" for the privilege of having a cabin for himself. He said that he would not leave, and a heated discussion ensued. He was very upset, and when I suggested that we could share the cabin, he got even more upset and stormed out of the cabin and disappeared. Since he did not return, I had the cabin to myself.

I later learned that my exiled cabin-mate had gone to the ticket office and vehemently complained. He apparently was so upset that he began shouting and threatening the folks selling tickets, and after trying unsuccessfully to calm him down they called the police. The police were also unsuccessful in calming him down and he caused such an uproar that he ended up in jail. I never did see him again.

The first part of the trip to Manaus was to cross the Bay of Marajo to reach the mouth of the Amazon River. The river near the mouth is very salty and was light yellow in color with a greenish tint. As we got underway into the bay we suddenly faced a strong wind that created white caps throughout. Until we got further up-river, it was a rather bumpy ride.

When we later sat down for dinner at the Captain's table, I discovered that the Captain was strongly Indian, short, medium built, taciturn. He went heavily for pepper in his food. Lunch consisted of three courses: one of fish with rice, one of beans and rice, and one of meat with rice. Rice was also the only side dish. All of it was very spicy. Everything at lunch was very formal and there was no conversation.

In the morning I awoke to find the jungle barely 100 yards away. The shoreline was heavily jungled, but this portion of the river was still subject to the ocean tide, every six hours. Although the area along the river was sparsely populated, I did occasionally see a small collection of houses, all built of wood and with small piers for small boats that carried goods for sale. The products, if any, consisted of alligator skins, fish, rubber, and fibers. And that first day I found very little bird life along the river; I saw only two large yellow butterflies.

At sunset, however, when the fish played in the quiet reaches, I detected the mystical cries of the night creatures. As light deepened into darkness, sounds of the jungle made one feel small and humble. Although I recognized some of the nighttime voices, most were entirely new to me. Most days on the river I saw only a few terns, an occasional cormorant, and a few parrots and parakeets. Their golden undersides glittering in the late sun. But perhaps the most exciting wild animals recorded there were the Amazon River dolphins that I found in small pods almost constantly. This species, sometimes known as gray or pink dolphin, due to its varied colors, is truly a fascinating creature. Those we encountered ranged from four to eight feet in length. And on one occasion I observed one with a surprisingly large fish being held side-wise in its long beak-like mouth. I was amazed when I saw its long rows of small but very sharp teeth that held that fish so firmly. I later learned that these river dolphins utilize ecolocation to locate prey.

By mid-morning of the next day the river floodplain was dominated by flat savannas covered with coarse grasses. Occasionally a wandering cowboy appeared, and cattle roamed the landscape. And just after dark on the third day we sighted the lights of Santarem, the principal town on the river between Belem and Manaus. In talking with one the *Florida* passengers, he told me that Santarem "is known for its excellent climate. It is a very healthy region and a popular vacation place."

Once we docked at Santarem, I watched as the stevedores unloaded a huge amount of goods, and they then loaded an even larger amount of produce. It seemed to me that the principal products of Santarem included cases or large sacks of cassava, malva, beans and rice. I struck up a conversation with one of the other observers, a local gentleman from his dress, who told me that the major trade products of the area included rosewood oil, rubber, jute, and lumber. He also told me that Santarem was founded in 1661 as a Jesuit Mission to a Tapago Indian settlement. And he also said that the town was earlier settled by a group of exiled Confederates from the U.S. Civil War. I did not see any evidence of the Confederacy during my short visit.

The next town along the river was Obidos, located at the narrowest part of the great river between Belem and Manaus. The town was hot and dry, and we stayed only long enough to unload a considerable amount of goods. There appeared little organization in the effort. It was left to several Indian stevedores who appeared to be fine specimens, full-blooded, strapping, though short of stature.

That night on the river I will long remember. It was a beautiful night. The river was motionless and clear, and a shimmering band of silver reflections accompanied us as we streamed along. There was a slight breeze blowing, and I spent much of the night on deck enjoying the night and the abundance of stars glimmering brightly overhead.

At Itacoatiara, we made a brief stop to unload and to acquire a few supplies. Itacoatiara has a reputation for being the birthplace of Petronilla Rodrigues, an Amazonian beauty once know far and wide. However, she had a very difficult life. One of our passengers told me that she "had been raped at fourteen, and she earned a living selling her body at the numerous small villages along the river. She was said that 'I sell my body, but there is no joy in it. I live only because it is so hard to die'." It was a strange statement that I would long remember.

Once we arrived in Manaus, I learned that there were no roads into the interior where I was to work. So I was given an office in town. Located on the confluence of the Negro and Solimaos Rivers, Manaus is considered to be the center of the Amazonian rainforest. It also is the capital of the Brazilian state of Amazonas, and Portuguese is the dominant language. And I learned to speak Portuguese very quickly, maybe because it was similar to Spanish that I already spoke so well. During my stay in Manaus, I discovered that the city was beautiful and contained magnificent buildings and parks. Plus, I found a couple of restaurants that served native food that I found delicious.

All during the time I worked for the rubber company we used enormous Catalina flying boats that could land on water. They could fly from Brazil to Miami without refueling, taking five tons of rubber with them. We flew them up and down, back and forth, all day long. There were 13 stations scattered throughout the interior and I was responsible for supplying those stations with food and bringing out rubber on the return trip. It was a marvelous opportunity for seeing the Amazon. Weekly I visited one or two of the 13 stations somewhere in the Amazon Valley.

My work also provided the opportunity to observe birds. I discovered that, at least in forested places where I was able to visit, it wasn't half as rich as Venezuela. It did, however, offer several unique species, like trumpeters, currasows, and tinnamous, and I found an amazing abundance of beautiful and unusual hummingbirds. They were of special interest.

I stayed down there all during the war, and when the rubber operation came to a close I found a job with the Wrigley Company, that operated the chewing gum business. It was very similar to rubber, and they were tickled to death to find someone who spoke both Spanish and Portuguese, and was already living there. I worked in Brazil, Venezuela, and San Salvador for Wrigley for almost four years.

I enjoyed living and working in both Brazil and Venezuela, and I also was much impressed with San Salvador; it was a great country for birds, particularly for hummingbirds. It seemed that every flower had a contingency of brightly-colored hummers, each one brighter than the last.

It also was there in San Salvador that I observed small snail-eating hawks. I would come across snail shells, some as large as three inches in length, scattered on the ground underneath large trees. Sometimes there was a large pile of shells, dropped there by the hawk that had perched in the overhead branches. That snail-eating hawk had a special bill for taking out the snail bodies. It was a funny looking hawk, rather plain, and when I approached it closer it would fly off and land in a nearby tree. It seemed almost unafraid. I was afforded excellent observations with binoculars.

Wrigley was very pleased with me, mainly because I was honest. I would go to the bank and draw as much money as needed; I paid for all the rubber and chewing gum that was brought in. I was buying thousands of pounds a week. They even sent me to Singapore to develop the chewing gum industry there. They gave me a house, salary, everything that I needed. I remained in Singapore for about six months with very few days off. Finally, one day I told the manager, "Sir, this is wonderful, and I love my work, but please, I've got jungle fever. I've been in jungles so much that I need a time off." I told him that "I need a different environment for a few days; I want to go Miami for at least two weeks." He immediately consented and I was soon en route to Miami. The Wrigley Company was very good to me. It was the best company I ever worked for.

I found Miami to be a delightful place. You could walk around at any hour. It was a great time of year, there was no crime, and I was able to see much of that city. Then I picked up an issue of the Miami Sunday Times that was devoted to the Virgin Islands. It told about marvelous things that were happening there. And being that close, with daily flights, I decided to go for a day or two to see my old house and a number of friends. Ramona had left me during my time in the Amazon, and had moved back to Santo Domingo with her relatives. She had missed her family and was not happy living in the jungle.

I had good intentions in Miami that, after visiting the Virgin Islands, to fly to New York and from there back to Singapore. But that was not to be. I met a childhood sweetheart, Betty Norman, in St. Thomas, who I had once been violently in love with, and she with me. But like many young people, we had quarreled one day over some silly thing, and she had marched off to Santo Domingo. I had not seen her since. But there she was, on the street in St. Thomas, and that is when the fireworks began. We were married almost immediately, and I told the Wrigley people that I wasn't going to return.

At first, I lived with Betty at her home in St. Thomas; I was very happy and our relationship was amazing. However, in a few weeks I met some government people who said: "My God, we've been looking for someone like you for months. We are starting a Fish and Wildlife Program for the Virgin Islands and we need someone to head it up. We have an office on St. Croix at a new Resource Center. Would you be interested? There is one catch," he added, "The job hardly pays anything." But I had found a girl again, and I didn't care much about whether there was good pay or not. I'm that kind of a bird. So, I said, "I'll take it." It was wildlife work and that was the hook.

Since I would live on St. Croix, I soon found a little house in Annas Hope that I could afford. That was an area I had always admired on account that it has a gut that runs though heavy forest where deer and blue pigeons abounded. However, it had a miserable dirt access road that took more than a month to repair before I had Betty join me. She soon had prepared the house as only women can do, and before long she found work with the Department of Agriculture. So we were then able to daily traveled to town together.

It felt extremely good to be back into my original homeland. I honestly believed that I would never leave.

Chapter 13

Not long after I went to work at St. Croix's Resource Center, I was introduced to Dr. James Sutton, the Center's principal scientist. Almost immediately we became extremely close; he was a brilliant man and became my mentor for the next several years. He taught me a great deal of what I learned about my job and also about the Virgin Islands environment. I had once thought that I had a pretty good handle on the Virgin Island's natural history, but there was much more to learn if I was to do my job. Largely because of Dr. Sutton and being back on my home turf, so to speak, I thoroughly enjoyed my job those first few years working for the Virgin Islands government. In addition, one of my assistances, Clark Hedges, and I hit if off extremely well.

I honestly felt extremely comfortable working with the wildlife on my homeland. I pretty well knew what to expect year-round. For instance, February was always the driest period. I had once called it "the month of purification, of the earth by the winds and the sun." April marked the nesting of leatherback sea turtles at Sandy Point and the migration of the Zenaida doves. And on a clear night, the Southern Cross appeared early and hung straight and bright above the southern coast. It also was the time when the stilts brought out their young and the martins begin arriving. All spring and summer our little yellow-breasts were active, singing their rasping but cheerful "zee-e-e-ie" songs and inspecting all our tables for what sugar they could discover. These little birds were the favorite of both mine and Betty's.

Before long my wife and I moved to a house that had a beautiful view and where I had more freedom to roam the countryside. Deer and blue pigeons were all over the place; it was wonderful. We used to go down to a little rocky pool with water like ice. Not a soul there, just the two of us. I was able to build the pool up, little by little, so that we could actually swim in that cold, cold water.

I would sit still near the pool and just enjoy the surroundings. I found that you can see more birds by sitting in one spot than by prowling over the hills all day. The warblers in particular, at certain times of the year, would all come in to drink. I saw more uncommon songbirds down there than all the walking around might produce.

At first my work kept me excited and busy. I was involved with surveys and studies of a wide variety of the native wildlife, especially the deer, quail and pigeons. I also was involved with protecting the wildlife from poachers. In fact, I risked my life several times defending deer from poachers. It sometimes seemed that the East End was alive with poachers. At night, people would walk up and down the roads and shoot those deer that came to the roadsides. They would then take it home to butcher or sell it to a friend running a butchershop. I spend many nights in the field, and Clark had one very close call with a poacher.

Clark and his assistants encountered a poacher on East End one day. Clark had met him there on a previous night and warned him about poaching, telling him that it was illegal to hunt deer at that time of year, and the next time he was encountered with a rifle he would be arrested. The man was a notorious character with a long police record. One night Clark again encountered the man carrying a rifle along the roadway, and when he told him he could not hunt that area at all, the poacher became belligerent, threatening Clark. He actually pointed the rifle at him. So Clark drew his Colt 22 automatic that he carried, and he shot him in the head. Killed him on the spot. Clark was later brought to trial and only because so many of his friends came to his rescue did he get off. But it was not a comfortable situation, and because most of the poacher's friends and family were locals, and many of them had threatened Clark, he resigned and moved off-island. He found a similar job on Antigua.

I soon understood that I was the lone voice protecting the wildlife. The island administrators didn't give a damn about poaching. I was unable to get a raise from what little salary I started with. Dr. Sutton understood my predicament. He told me that the administration "has no interest what-so-ever in birdlife or conservation." And when I eventually asked my boss for a raise, I was told "why should you receive a raise when you are doing exactly what you want." He looked me straight in the face and said, "Greg, you don't seem to realize you are the only man in government that is being paid for his hobby."

I never got a raise. I was making the same salary after 22 years that I started with. But before I left my employment I was asked to interview and then train my replacement, which I did. That man started at almost twice the salary that I had been making.

My quarterly reports, that were required to be on time, didn't seem to conform to what they wanted. I would write on deer, quail or pigeons, or even write some nonsense, and I received barely any response. I came to believe that my reports were not even read. They were placed on a shelf to prove to whoever was their supervisor that something was being done.

However, because of my interest and knowledge of conservation of the natural resources, I was asked to write a "Conservation Master Plan for the U.S. Virgin Islands." At first I was surprised that they had asked me, but then I realized no one else had the personal knowledge of the diversity of the islands. No one else could prepare something like a conservation plan. I was happy to do so. I worked very hard on that plan, visiting all of the key resources within the area, including the many off-shore cays. I realized that this project was a very special opportunity to emphasize the unique resources available throughout the Virgin Islands.

That plan also provided me an opportunity to visit the Salt River Bay area, one of the most valuable resources anywhere in the Caribbean. I actually was able to visit the Salt River area on several occasions. Just when I thought that I knew the area pretty well, something more was said about its significance that allowed me to go back again. I knew no other area that contained such important natural and culture resources, all within about five square miles.

My comprehensive plan was developed in such a way to address all of the island's threatened and endangered species by long-range monitoring, management of the deer populations, control of mongoose and rat populations, and develop a program to control shoreline erosion. The various projects would address the potential declines of several of the most threatened wildlife, such as sea turtles and the endemic St. Croix ground-lizard.

I wrote in summary that "We must lay aside suitable areas now for the protection of the native flora and fauna if tomorrow's population is to have and enjoy it. Our countryside can be urbanized out of all beauty and recreational value in an astonishingly short time. One look around and it is alarmingly evident that the scenic beauty of all the islands is at stake."

But like my quarterly reports, my Conservation Plan, that I had worked on so long and so hard, was also shelved. I became very wearisome about the Island administrators ignoring the resources they were responsible for protecting.

Within my Plan I used the condition of Krause Lagoon as one example of changes brought about by the over use by humans. Over the years I observed that many of the areas that I once considered rather pristine were being degraded by excessive human traffic. Krause Lagoon was once a magnificent little everglades. The 600 acres was a resting place for thousands of migratory birds. It was the only place clapper rails occurred; they nested there. Hearing them in the afternoons was truly special. And it was the only place where least bitterns lived. They had beautiful green eggs, and nested in little bunches of reeds within the mangroves. I would see them fly into the reeds and put their necks up like they were looking straight up.

Ruddy ducks also laid there. They laid a perfectly round egg, so big that you would think that it was from a goose. You would wonder how it was possible that a little duck could possibly produce such an egg. The most common shorebirds found were the willets and stilts. What a loud and obnoxious birds they were.

And Krause Lagoon was the home of hundreds of pairs of white-crowned pigeons. They would arrive in spring and leave in September. I've banded more than 1100 white-crowned pigeons there. They also are resident in the Sugar Bay mangroves. But many of the best mangrove stands have declined in recent years, all the result of overdelopment.

I had earlier conducted a series of bird counts in the Salt River mangroves, one of the best mangroves in all the Virgin Islands. Red, black and white mangroves occur there within the approximately 13 acres. Individual bird numbers found on my counts during the fall months ranged from a low of 39 on October 1 to a high of 161 on October 26, the peak of the Caribbean fall migration. A total 35 species were recorded, but 15 of those were full-time resident. The remaining 17 species occur there only during migration and/ or in winter. Fourteen warblers resided there throughout the winter months. Most numerous warblers included the yellow, prairie, and black-and-white warblers and American redstart, northern waterthrush, and northern parula.

My monthly reports included a diversity of wildlife topics. A few included life history studies of white-crowned pigeons and Zenaida doves, as well as food habits of pigeons, doves, and the bridled quail-dove. The bridled quail-dove was of special interest because that species is found only on a few

Caribbean Islands, from Puerto Rico southward into the Leeward Island, and nowhere else. It is a mid-sized, illusive and shy bird that lives in the dense woodlands with thick undergrowth. The bridled quail-dove is endemic to that small part of the world.

As a boy, living primarily in the lowlands with the sugar cane crops and in the town of Fredricksted, I did not know of the bridled-quail dove. My good friend Johnny was first to bring it my attention after he discovered one along the Creque Dam Road. Later Johnny showed one to me on one of our excursions on Blue Mountain. The reason it was little known and usually ignored because it was not a popular huntable species. Yet, I found it one of the most interesting of all our birds because of its unusual behavior. Although it spends a good deal of time walking about in the shady undergrowth, it can often be found sitting on upper branches of shrubs. I found that I could approach it fairly close before it would fly down to the ground and waddle away. And its song is a very low "who-whooo," so low that many folks can not hear it.

In addition, I wrote papers on the deer on St. Croix, the life history of the pearly-eyed thrasher, and the concept of stocking Guineafowl, chachalacas, white-winged doves, and bobwhites. Many St. Croix citizens wanted us to introduce a variety of huntable species, including pheasants, and they wrote letters to the administration about their wishes. But it did not happen, primarily because I was able to talk some sense. I convinced my supervisors that the introduction of exotics would very likely negatively effect our native populations. It was one of the few issues that I won.

I did, however, introduce chachalacas to both St. Croix and St. Thomas. I thought it was the one bird that might make it, since it didn't live on the ground and likes dry scrub country. I got 20 birds from Columbia. But I found out that chachalacas domesticate at the drop of a hat. They very easily domesticate. And apparently when they are first introduced into a new habitat they have trouble finding food. So whenever they found a flock of Guineafowl or chickens, where somebody would throw out corn, they would then go to feed there again and again. And they were promptly shot and eaten. The locals found them quite edible. I really thought if they had been left alone they would have done well. The last one on St. Croix was found near Frediksted and shot.

I also brought in 400 California quail, because they could nest on low shrubs and roost in bushes, and not be subject to mongoose predation. And inside of a year there wasn't one. The locals found quail delicious.

They also shot Zenaida doves whenever possible. There was a yearly migration of these doves that came in from the west. Don't ask me where. They came in for weeks about Easter time, the reason they were called "Easter doves." Some remained on the islands, but other kept going to wherever. St. Croix never had the dove numbers as St. Thomas did. One day I counted 10,000 Zenaida doves passing St. Thomas. From daylight to sunset they streamed across in small flocks.

I took a plane one afternoon and followed them awhile before we turned back, but the doves kept going east. It was incredible the amount of Zenaida doves that migrated through these islands in April and the beginning of May. Apparently they do the same thing on other Caribbean islands.

My overall impression about saving the key resources on St. Croix was that it was too late to save many of the best bird viewing areas, such as Caledonia, Eagle Mountain and a few others. The resident birds had taken a heavy toll due to non-native predators, especially mongooses. They are deadly on ground-nesting birds and lizards, even the iguanas. Plus, declines are also related to introduced chemicals to the cane fields. In the early days the only fertilizer used was from cattle, mules and horses. But when they began spraying biocides they killed the broadleaf plants and also cleaned out the insects that many of the smaller birds, such as flycatchers and warblers, depended upon. Even some waterbirds, like the herons, shorebirds and ducks, were affected.

It seemed that over the years, after writing so many reports and preparing a truly comprehensive conservation plan, being either personally or my recommendations being ignored, that I lost faith in the system. There were days when I could hardly go to work and do my job.

I finally left the Virgin Island Government with sadness. During the 20-odd years that I had with the local government, in the field in which I worked, I didn't get to first base. It was very unsatisfactory from the standpoint of having built a feeling among the people of the islands relative to conservation. I did everything possible. I never got to first base. They were not interested.

And yet, years after not "getting to first base" while working for the government as a lone voice for natural resource protection, many of my initial recommendations were implemented. St. Croix's north shore was established as a national wildlife refuge to protect nesting leatherback sea turtles, Green Cay, off St. Croix's north shore, was established as a national wildlife refuge to protect the last remnants of the endangered St. Croix ground-lizard, and the Virgin Island Legislature passed a Territorial Parks Act to protect other places of biological importance. But the one most significant site in all the Virgin Islands that did not get fully protected was Salt River Bay. There was too much interest from developers there to give it full protection. It took many years before that site was recognized by the National Park Service and established as the Salt River Bay Historical Park and Ecological Preserve.

I went into retirement with many, many unbelievable and marvelous memories of my years enjoying nature in all parts of the world. And I soon found myself writing short stories about those many experiences, and finally I wrote a novel that included my many adventures as well as many of my other life experiences.